KING OF DECEPTION

LORDS OF LAS VEGAS

TAMMY ANDRESEN

❀ Created with Vellum

A GIFT FOR YOU!

Want a FREE novella? More from the Lords of Las Vegas series? Join my newsletter and get King Daddy as my gift to you!

KING OF DECEPTION

A powerfully cunning aristocratic billionaire
A sacrificial princess

I might have had one too many glasses of champagne during my getaway bachelorette party.

It's the hazard of toasting a wedding that feels like a life sentence.

But when I stumble into the wrong hotel room, I run smack into the most sinfully delicious man I've ever laid eyes on…

Gris looks like a dream.
Gorgeous.
Sexy.
And the accent...

It doesn't matter that I'm a virgin.
Or that my family's business is at stake.

It's my deepest, most delicious fantasy come to life.

The problem, though?

Gris isn't a dream. He's a nightmare.

The devil in disguise.

Because he isn't just some random stranger.

He is my family's greatest enemy.

Our Las Vegas real estate rival.

He knows exactly who I am.

He knows my biggest secret and how to use me to take everything my family has built.

And I walked right into his trap.

CHAPTER ONE

Arabella

I step away from the circle of light surrounding the beachside bar and draw a deep breath of ocean air as the darkness surrounds me.

Finally, I can breathe.

I'd normally find an oceanside resort on the island of Maui fun, or at least relaxing. But not this time.

"Bella, come back!" Cici yells from her stool on the bar. "We're just getting started!"

"You go ahead," I call back to Cici and Maggie, who already have several men vying for their attention. They'll honestly have more fun without me. "Put your drinks on Mason's tab."

My champagne flute is still in my hand. I'm not much of a drinker, and I think this might be my third.

My friends kept ordering them for me. I didn't have the heart to tell them the last thing I feel like doing is celebrating.

The diamond on my finger catches a bit of light from the nearby beachside bungalows, making the stone sparkle, further mocking me and my mood.

What would happen if I twisted the three-carat monstrosity off my finger and tossed it into the ocean?

My fiancé would likely just buy me another. The ring is, for sure, insured. He's not letting me slip away from this match that easily.

Preston Wingate III is the kind of old money that only highlights the fact that my family is a bunch of hustlers.

My father was a gangster. My brothers try to hide the truth from me about what he did for a living, but I still know. Our father worked for the Italian Mafia until it killed him.

And I actually mean killed him. Not like he had a heart attack from work stress. He was murdered by mob boss Toni Carcetti.

My brothers are still mucking around with illegal dealings, though they try to share as little as possible about that side of the business with me too. My oldest brother, Mason, has a whole legal real estate development front that is growing stronger. He owns several casinos on the Las Vegas strip, clubs, and apartment buildings. Recently, he built a tunnel that connects them all, funneling the foot traffic to our companies, keeping them within our businesses. It's brilliant.

But the costs have left him vulnerable. Enter Preston Wingate. Mason swears that with my fiancé's help, he can shed the last of our illegal dealings, and place us so far above our competition, we become untouchable, making our family safe.

Preston's connections will infuse us with enough money and friends in high places that my brothers can finally stop being gangsters.

Which would be wonderful because the danger has always been a breath away.

As if that isn't enough, five men all with alpha-type personalities running one company can get… complicated.

They haven't told me what happened a few months ago. But I know it was something big. Because my cousin, who is really like my brother, wants out. Luke is selling his shares.

Mason's buying them, of course. He never misses a business trick. But in a twist I didn't see coming, he's putting them in my name.

Something about needing to diversify shares for the board. I don't know.

They sent me to New York to go to school. It was for my protection. But now, I've been drawn right back into the web that is our family's business.

I'm willing to help. I am. I want Mason to go legit. I want Luke to be happy. But the price, the plan to make all this happen is for me to marry Preston.

Which seemed easy at first. Handsome. Charming. He's everything I should want. And best of all, he's old money, the kind with names and connections.

We met at a gallery opening. There was an instant connection, or so I thought. But it burned out quick. He's so stuffy, and I'm not sure I'm enough for him…

I stumble as I cross the lawn. Each beachside bungalow has sweeping water views, each cute and posh, but they all look exactly alike. I pause for a moment. Which one was mine? Third over? Or was it the fourth?

Drawing in a deep breath, I start forward again. I'm not worried. I left my French doors open, no one in a place like this steals from an unlocked room.

But it also means everyone has left their doors open too.

Stopping, I scrunch my brows and search the cute little buildings with their front porches and steps right into the sand.

I was the third… I'm sure of it.

Swallowing down my last bit of champagne, I start up the two steps and set my glass down on the porch table. I slip my heels off the moment I reach the top of the stairs.

Reaching down, I grab the straps, so they're dangling from a finger as I make my way inside.

A single small lamp by the bed is on, and I don't bother to turn on more lights as I move to the dresser, dropping my shoes.

My black suitcase is in the corner, just where I left it.

I slip off my earrings, setting them on top of the entertainment console, then do the same with the monster ring.

A sigh escapes my lips to have the thing off. I'd rethink my decision to marry Preston, but I don't know how to even start the conversation.

When he asked, part of me was relieved. I didn't want to be part of the business, but I also didn't want to let my brothers down. Preston could handle Kincaid Enterprises for me. The arrangement seemed ideal.

And then there is Mason. He's beyond thrilled to welcome Preston into the fold.

My fiancé brings us a legitimacy that Mason has always wanted, and further protection from our enemies. Mason has already started attending the country club events with Preston and has possible deals with several of Preston's friends.

I shake my head, my eyes sliding closed. Everything started happening so fast… before I knew it, invitations were being sent out, and dresses were being picked and…

I'm not sure Preston loves me any more than I love him. In fact, I think he might like me less.

But what he has in connections, I have in money. Something he and his family have been lacking of late. Not that you'd know it by his lifestyle.

The Wingates have the best of everything.

I pinch the bridge of my nose. Remembering my chain of logic doesn't help soothe my growing unrest. At twenty-two, this isn't how I saw my life going. A marriage of convenience to finance an underground Las Vegas tunnel.

I was studying fashion in New York, talking about getting a job with a designer, working my way up the corporate ladder. And I was making progress…

But there is no going back now.

Unclipping my bracelet watch that Luke gave me for Christmas, I turn toward the bathroom. My head is spinning from the champagne and all I want to do is fall asleep.

But that's when I realize the bathroom light is on. Did I leave it on? Cocking my head, I pull my dark brown hair over one shoulder, reaching the zipper at the back of my dress. The zipper slides smoothly open, the dress slumping forward.

I just want to brush my teeth and collapse into bed.

But when I reach for the bathroom door, cracking it open, a plume of steam comes out. I blink a few times, trying to understand. I didn't leave the water running, did I?

That's when the door opens wider.

I gasp, taking a step back, my eyes going wide.

Standing before me, backlit by the bathroom light, is a nearly naked man. The light highlights the glistening breadth of his shoulders, the narrow taper of his waist, the long, lean length of him.

Taking another step back, a squeaking scream tumbles from my lips.

He steps out of the bathroom, the towel around his hips, slung low enough that I can see the cut of his muscle at his hip.

Because all the light is behind him, I can't make out his face, but he can see mine. I start to scream again, my hands coming to my face.

He straightens. "I don't know what you're doing here, but usually people who break into other people's rooms aren't the ones who scream."

My mouth drops open as it takes me at least three seconds longer than it should to process those words. Maybe it's the posh British accent that slows my understanding, or maybe it's the champagne, but suddenly I realize… I'm in the wrong room!

My face flames. Spinning, I bump right into the bed, my shin clonking the frame as I gasp out in pain.

I'm skittering to the side, apologies tumbling from my lips, as I half hop and nearly trip in my effort to collect my things.

"I'm so sorry—" I say for the fourth time and then trip over my own shoes.

I feel myself falling but I'm too intoxicated to catch myself. That's the exact moment strong arms circle my torso, and suddenly, I stop halfway to the floor, my front pressed to a rock-hard chest.

My eyes go wide as my hands bite into flexing biceps. I mean… wow.

Snapping my chin up, my lips part in surprise. I'm staring into the dark brown depths of the most sinfully beautiful eyes I've ever seen. Or maybe it's just his whole face.

Straight nose, strong cheekbones, a jaw that could cut glass. The only thing soft is his mouth, and my God, heat floods between my legs as I stare at that mouth. I'd like for those lips to devour me.

Wait. How long have we been like this? With me suspended halfway between standing and the floor. "I… I'm… I'm so sorry," I rasp out, my voice taking on this sultry tone I've never heard before. "I'll just get my things and…"

He quirks a half smile as his hands spread out on my back. Is he tired of holding me like this?

He doesn't seem it, his features completely relaxed. "Or…" The smile grows. "You could stay."

My mouth drops open, as I struggle to form a coherent thought. Did he just offer to... to… I'm afraid to even finish the sentence in my head.

Even before Preston, I barely dated.

It's part of having three overprotective brothers who are always worried about my safety. And there is the whole *their enemy killed our father* thing.

Worried about me being alone in New York, they assigned me a security detail when I went away to college. A guy discreetly followed me to class, out at night. I was never alone, and I was always being watched. So, unlike most of my friends, I've never done a one-night stand before. I've never done anything before.

"I couldn't," I whisper, my mouth dry, my hands digging deeper into his skin like they're in complete revolt of my words. They don't seem to want to let him go.

He slowly pulls me to standing, but he doesn't let me out of his embrace. If anything, one of his hands slides lower, to the place just above my rear end, pressing the cradle of my hips deeper into his. The ache between my legs gives a throb.

"Suit yourself," he murmurs, his mouth moving closer to mine. It's like he's hypnotizing me. My eyes flutter closed as I try to collect my wits. "Name's Gris."

"Bella," I answer, my fingers on my left hand unlock enough to slide up his arm until they reach his shoulder, my thumb settling in the deep cut of his collarbone.

"Nice to meet you, Bella," he replies and then his lips brush over mine in this featherlight kiss that is so soft, I wonder if I dreamed it.

"You too?" I return, my eyes still closed. When they finally open, I realize he's straightened up and I feel heat completely flood my cheeks once again. How long have I been hanging on the precipice of another kiss?

His hands slide to my sides and then trace down over the curve of my hips as he lowers himself into a crouch.

The towel parts with the bend of his legs and I can almost see his… I swallow down a lump, realizing, even as I'm trying to catch a peek of his junk, that his face is just in front of my…

I'm already aching between the legs, but at the proximity of his mouth, I feel the flood of moisture and I can actually smell my arousal in the air.

Which means he can smell me too. He looks up at me with another wicked grin before he grabs my shoes and stands back up.

My hands are on both his shoulders now. When did I reach for him with my other hand? I can't bring myself to stop touching him, apparently. He places the strappy three-inch sandals between us. "You'll need these then."

"Right," I say with a tiny nod. *Get it together, Arabella,* I give myself a mental shake as I let go of one of his shoulders and reach for the shoes, our fingers brushing.

I just need to collect my things, slink out the door, die of embarrassment, and then figure out how to use the shower head in my own room to relieve the ache between my legs.

But as I take the shoes, I look down and see the sparkle of my engagement ring on the top of Gris's console. The ring is a D color, VS1 clarity, set in a six-prong platinum setting. It's perfectly cold and the idea of putting it back on my finger makes me shiver.

I look back up at the man that I'm still holding with one hand. Drawing in a deep breath of air, I lick my lips. "What are the rules if I did stay?"

Oh, the way he looks at me. It's deliciously wicked and I want to dive into sin without looking back. "What do you want them to be?"

He isn't serious? I swallow down a lump, the intensity of his stare makes the words die on my tongue. He's very serious.

"I..." I lick my lips again as he watches the path of my tongue, his dark brown eyes growing ever darker. "I can't have sex with you."

One of his brows quirks up. Does he know it's because I have another guy? The ring is right there.... I bet he hasn't guessed that it's because I've never done this. And I don't just mean the one-night stand.

I've never done any of it. I've never had sex before.

"All right then. What about kissing?" he asks his voice dropping low, with the kind of heat that has me getting even wetter.

"Yes," I gasp a moment before he leans in, taking my mouth in a much firmer and deliberate press of his lips.

"How about here?" And then he bends a bit to place his lips on the fluttering pulse of my neck.

"Yes."

"Here?" he asks, planting another full-mouthed kiss in the middle of my chest.

My head tips back. "Yes."

His hands come to the back of my dress, still open from when I unzipped it. I'm not really big-chested, but I'm not small either. A solid C-cup with breasts that are high and perky so I can go without a bra if the dress is right.

Which I did tonight.

The fabric of my cotton eyelet dress brushes down my shoulders and pools around my waist as he drops lower, his lips hovering just over one of my nipples. I can feel his warm breath on the sensitive skin, the proximity of his lips already making my nipple pucker. "Here?"

My head tips further back as I arch my chest up.

"Yes."

He sucks one nipple between his lips, his tongue swirling over the pebbled skin and I cry out, burying my hands in his hair. I've never been the most sexual person. It honestly scared me. Until tonight.

Because with him...

It's like he flipped some switch.

But he isn't done, not even close. He moves to the other breast, giving it equal attention before he slides lower. "Here?"

"Yes."

He licks at the skin of my stomach, tonguing my belly button before he tugs the dress lower, until it clears my hips and drops to the floor.

I'm only in my thong and I might be embarrassed, but he stops his mouth an inch from the V between my legs. "Here?"

Even the idea of him kissing me where I ache has me sighing out a moan. "Yes." The way I say it, I might as well be begging.

If he stopped now, I'm pretty sure I would.

CHAPTER TWO

Arabella

Fortunately for me, Gris doesn't stop. He tips forward the slightest bit and plants a kiss right on my sensitive clit, still covered in my thong as another moan falls from my lips.

His tongue slides over the fabric and I hold onto his hair the way a cowgirl might hold the mane of a horse.

The strands are still damp from his shower, his cologne and natural woodsy scent filling my nostrils as I try to keep from whimpering out my begging pleas.

Hooking one of my legs over his shoulder, he places another kiss right where I need it most and then sucks on my clit.

It's like liquid fire shoots through me.

I had no idea that one man could turn me into this. Melt all my inhibitions in a matter of seconds, but here I am.

The ache pulses through me and I flex my hips to give him even more access. I don't want him to stop.

But he's done asking me what I want as he stands.

I cry out my protest anyway, even as he wraps an arm around my waist and lifts me up off the floor.

I've never been naked in a man's arms like this before and it's amazing, the warm roughness of his skin against mine.

I wrap my arms around his neck, and he buries his other hand in my hair, cradling my head, as he tips my face down so that he can kiss my lips.

Using his mouth, he guides my lips apart, his tongue plunging into mine.

It's hot and sexy as our tongues tangle. I'm not so naïve that I've never kissed a man before. But I have never been kissed like this. I can feel the heat between my legs spiraling out of control just from the press of our bodies and his kiss.

I don't even notice he's carried me across the room until he lowers me to the bed. If I thought his skin felt good when we were standing, when his weight comes down on top of me, I let out this long breathy moan.

He's turned me into the most wanton woman...

But he's kissing down my body again, and this time, when he gets to my belly, he fists either side of my thong, pulling it down over my hips.

I have one moment where I know he's going to see what no man has before, but I can barely think about it, before his lips come down over my clit and he sucks it into his mouth. Without the cloth, it feels even better, though it's sensitive enough that I bite at my lip, a little bit of pain mixing with the pleasure.

But he isn't done. He wraps his fingers under my knee, opening me wider to him before his hand slides up my thigh, and then he uses his fingers to spread my lips open.

The way he's touching me, confident, in command, it just makes me hotter as I chase his tongue with my hips.

And then he slides a finger inside me. I feel myself tighten around him. Grip him. But he feels so good inside me, my back arches, my hair sliding on the bed as I thrash back and forth, whimpering

He eases back, and I push up to look at him, about to beg for his touch. The look in his eyes makes my breath catch. It's so possessive it's almost predatorial.

"You like that, luv?"

"Please," I plead, my fingers sliding into his hair again, tightening my grip on the strands. "Please don't stop."

He looks me at me for one more second, and I swear, he's like a lion about to devour his prey before he dives back in, licking me exactly where I need it.

I feel the pleasure knotting so tightly that my back arches again, my toes curling, one fist clenching in the sheets, the other in his hair.

And then I break apart, shattering into a thousand tiny pieces as I cry out his name.

He slows his tongue but doesn't stop, his finger still buried inside me. My chest is heaving and I'm not sure I can see straight, but I can still feel as he starts kissing a path back up my body.

He doesn't remove his finger from inside me, though, his palm cupping my sex.

"In this arrangement of ours..." he growls out, his smooth accent making my inside walls clench around him again. "Do you return the favor?"

I lick my lips, drawing in a deep breath. Do I want to taste him? Feel him? "Yes."

I hear his rumble of approval a moment before my body is turning. He both pulls me on my side and spins me so I'm lined up with my mouth pointed toward his hips where he kneels in a crouch.

All while never taking his finger out of me.

The man has skills.

If I was ever going to do this... have one night of wild passion, I picked the right guy. It's so easy, I barely have to think.

With his free hand, he gives the towel a quick jerk and suddenly his cock is there in front of me.

My lips part as my eyes grow wide. Maybe I should have inspected the goods before I committed to the blowjob. I'm at the beginner level and even I know he is not beginner-sized.

He must sense my hesitation. With one hand still cupping between my legs, his finger inside me, he wraps a hand around the back of my head, his fingers gliding through my curtain of hair.

Slowly, he pulls me closer, and I lick my lips before I part them, letting the tip slide into my mouth.

My tongue darts out and I taste the smallest pearl of salty liquid. I've heard girls say it's gross, but I find it… kind of amazing.

I don't think delicious is the right word, but for some reason, I want more. It's just like him. Strong. Masculine. I sink my lips further down him, tentatively exploring.

"You ever done this before, Bella?"

I wince, knowing that he can tell. But he doesn't look upset as he pushes deeper into my mouth.

If anything, the cords of his neck stand out as he fists my hair tighter. I like that too. I think I would let this man do all manners of dirty and depraved things to me and that thought makes me sink even further, my lips wrapped around him until he hits the back of my throat.

And then, I don't know why, I hold. I like him filling me. I swear, I want to let him fill other places, not just my mouth.

We've barely started and he groans his approval, his head falling back, before he pulls my hair to slide his cock back out of my mouth. I come off with a pop, a little drool connecting my lip to the tip.

"Just like that," he grunts, pushing back into my mouth. "You're a natural."

Is he just saying that? I forget to worry as he hits the back of my throat again. "Hollow out your cheeks."

Is it weird that he's teaching me to do this? Give a blowjob?

But I do as he commands, letting him guide me with his hand at the base of my skull.

His left hand is flexing against my scalp, his right still cupping my sex, his finger inside me. I can feel his body tightening, his cock lengthening and thickening in my mouth.

I swear, it's making me hotter, and my body is rising to meet his. My hips start rocking against his hand as I tighten around his finger.

"Fuck, Bella," he growls, pumping in and out of me. "You're so tight."

I sink even further down on him, tears starting to stream from my eyes as I he fills my mouth with his cock.

It's like I can't get enough. I think I'm trying to take as much of him as possible while I have this chance. Or maybe it's because I know I'll never see him again.

I know what this is, Gris is not my Prince Charming. Just like I know what waits for me back home. But in this moment, I want as much of him as I can get.

I feel the current of energy that runs through him, I know he's close. I'm getting close too, my body beginning to shake as my second orgasm grows and swells.

I close my eyes, sliding up and down his thick shaft until he explodes in my mouth. I swallow him down, too far gone to even care, as my own body erupts in another orgasm.

I can't even cry out, but my eyes roll back, my body shuddering.

He pulls out of my mouth, his lips crashing down over mine, the kiss a sloppy mess. The orgasm was amazing. The kiss nearly as good.

I have no idea how men usually act after they cum, but I think it might be a good sign that I did all right since his tongue is in my mouth, his hand still wrapped between my legs, his finger inside me.

"Arabella," he rasps low and deep.

I look up at him, my brow furrowing. Something isn't right.

But he kisses me again, his finger slowly withdrawing from inside my body.

And then he wraps his arms around me, pulling me up the bed and settling me into the cradle of his arms under the covers.

I sigh, snuggling deep into his embrace.

I have no idea how one-night stands usually go. Is snuggling generally part of the equation?

Part of me thinks I should offer to leave. Slink off to my room with some part of my dignity. But part of me is ridiculously comfortable.

His muscular body has wrapped mine in a cocoon of warmth and security.

"That was amazing," I sigh out, my eyes closing.

"It was," he chuckles against my ear, kissing the sensitive spot on my neck. "You were."

I grin, already in that place between wakefulness and sleep. "I'm pretty sure if one of us was the catalyst of the quality, that was you."

He chuckles low and soft. "Sleep, luv. You must be exhausted."

I do. I fall asleep in the warmth of his embrace.

But I wake a little while later, my sleep-addled mind aware that I'm alone in the bed.

The bathroom light is still on. I lift up searching the room for Gris, but I can't find him. I lay my head back down, closing my eyes. Just as I drift off, I hear Gris's lilting voice say two words…

"It's done."

CHAPTER THREE

ARABELLA

I WAKE WITH A START, sitting up to the morning sun that's streaming through the French doors.

I have no idea what time it is, which is weird. Even on vacation, I usually wake like clockwork.

Pushing up, I realize I'm also naked. Another oddity. And then the details of the night flood back.

I find myself pulling up the covers, though I needn't have bothered. No one is here. I'm alone in the room. I grab the top sheet and wrap it around myself as I get up from the bed, my clothes neatly folded in one of the chairs that flank the couch in the sitting area. Each of the bungalows is set up like a studio apartment.

My stuff is still on the console, including the ring. Did Gris notice? Does it matter? There is no note, no evidence I didn't dream the entire encounter, except for the fact that this is clearly not my room.

I step into the bathroom, rinse my face and pull on my dress, collecting the rest of my stuff.

Stepping outside, I easily find my room in the light of day. Sighing, I push open the closed doors.... I thought I'd left them open...

But inside the air-conditioned space, I see my phone sitting on my console, lit up as it rings on silent.

Picking it up, I glance at the screen with a wince. I've got twenty missed calls.

Shit.

"Hello?" I say as I bring the phone to my ear.

"Where the fuck have you been?" my brother Mason rumbles into the phone. "I've called six times."

I look down at the phone, realizing that Cici and Maggie have been calling too. "I had the ringer off. I overslept."

"Overslept?" He growls, sounding very annoyed. "You never oversleep."

"You left the girls an open bar tab. They insisted I partake."

He grunts some form of agreement, his own culpability making him more amenable. "Got it." Then he clears his throat, moving on. "The reason I've been calling is because I need you to come home today."

"Today?" I cry, pulling the phone away from my ear. "But I just got here."

"Preston's parents have decided to come to Vegas to meet all of us. They're going to attend the charity event tonight for our new nonprofit, which is perfect, but it will require your attendance."

I let out a long breath of air. With each passing day, I get caught a little deeper in the web.

I try to remember how Preston and I ended up here. Not how we got engaged. But the first few dates. He seemed interested the first few times we went out, but when he made a major move on dates three and four and I resisted, he seemed to lose interest.

I honestly thought he was getting bored, but when I was called back to Vegas by Mason, and we faced a long-distance relationship, he proposed instead of breaking it off.

At first, I was thrilled. But instead of growing more invested, more loving after the engagement, I swear, he likes me less and less.

I'd only met his parents once in the short time we were dating, and I did not get the impression they liked me either.

I'm sure they consider my family nouveau riche at best.

"Preston's parents?" I ask shaking my head.

"That's right. It's ridiculously important this goes well. His father has the kind of friends…"

"Why…" I ask, ignoring Mason's networking opportunities. I'm tired of hearing about them. "Didn't my fiancé call me to tell me about his parents' visit?" I'd just looked through my list of missed calls. Preston was not one of them.

Not that I needed another reason to know that my engagement is all wrong. I stare down at the ring on my finger.

Maybe Mason can end this engagement for me. If he has to call me to tell me the Wingates are visiting, perhaps he can also call Preston and tell him we're not getting married. It seems fair.

"I'm the one ordering the jet," Mason answers as if that explains it. He must know it doesn't. He recently married and no other man, not even Charlotte's family, would care for Charlotte's needs in place of Mason.

He loves his wife to the point of distraction. It consumes him.

"Listen, Mason…" I start, my breath shaky as I draw in a lung full of air. "I don't think this—"

"Just come home. We'll talk about it when you get here."

I hang up, taking several deep gulps before I call to order breakfast and then head into the bathroom.

That's when a knock sounds at my door. Turning I see my friends standing outside my room, looking irritated.

Cici's got her hands on her hips and Maggie is glaring.

Shit.

I wave them in, Cici opening the door. "What the fuck?"

I wince. "Sorry."

Maggie's shrewd gaze travels up and down me. "You just did the walk of shame."

"What?" I gasp, knowing I've been caught. My college girlfriends would do this sort of thing all the time. Meet a guy, go home with him, come home the next day in the clothes they'd worn out the night before.

But they aren't engaged with their family business tied to their impending marriage. I'm the worst kind of person.

Cici's mouth falls open... "But you don't have sex. Have you and Preston even..."

Maggie cuts her off, flipping her auburn hair over her shoulder. "Preston doesn't matter." Then she turns back to me. "But where you slept last night does. Spill it."

"It's not like that," I push out weakly. But I've got to get it together. No one can know about last night, not even my friends. "Preston and I haven't, and I certainly didn't give my virginity to a stranger at a hotel."

Maggie looks skeptical, but Cici smiles in relief. She pulls her blonde hair off her neck. "I didn't think so. You're so lucky to have Preston, why would you cheat?"

Maggie snorts. She's a tall, gorgeous redhead that men fall over themselves to be with. "Preston is lucky to have her. Not that he seems to notice." I can tell she wants to say more. I've been sensing that Maggie doesn't like Preston, but she hasn't told me why and I haven't told her about my fears and reservations over the marriage. Once I let those words out, there will be no taking them back.

She steps closer to me, close enough, I find myself holding my breath. Then she takes a long sniff. "You smell like men's cologne and sex."

My eyes bug out. "I didn't..."

"Bullshit."

I lean in closer to Maggie, "I didn't sleep with him. I just..."

She purses her lips. "Let's get down to it. Is it just me or are you hating this engagement?"

The words nearly rush out of me. *Yes, I hate it. I want out. I want out right now.* But so much is at stake.

"Mags," I plead. "I'm working on it."

She lets out a giant rush of air, her shoulders wilting. "I'm so glad you are," she whispers close to my ear. "You shouldn't marry him, Bella, and I'm worried."

I reach for her hand then as Cici comes to stand next to Mags. "Are you going to tell us about the guy last night, or what?"

I shake my head. I know Maggie is right. I need to find a way out. I hope I can find a way out. But it's delicate. And if Mason or Preston learns the truth of what I'd just done, this entire situation could blow up in my face.

Mason is counting on me, and I've made promises to Preston.

Why did I make promises to Preston again? I rub my forehead. "No," I murmur as I drop my hand and shake my head. The less they know the better, and maybe I'll be able to control this whole situation.

An image of Gris rises in front of my eyes. Naked, powerful. My body throbs with need even though I just left his bed.

Oh man.

I've messed this one up good.

Convincing my friends to continue the trip without me, I get in the shower and get myself ready. I do full hair and makeup in case I don't have any time when I arrive back in Vegas.

I have no idea what I'm walking into, so I put on my war paint.

My long dark hair is styled in lose waves, as shiny as I can get them.

My makeup is natural, highlighting my cheekbones, I have good ones, and big brown eyes.

I go for a soft gloss that highlights the pale pink of my lips. For a dress, I only have so many options, but I brought a black wrap and I put it on, slipping into heels right before a knock sounds at the door.

That would be the driver…

Grabbing my suitcase with a sigh, I make my way to the door.

A man in a black suit stands outside the door. He takes my bags and leads me to the discreet black corporate car that's parked by reception. Opening my door, he helps me in before he loads the bags in the trunk.

I sigh out my irritation. I didn't want to celebrate, but I want to go back to Vegas even less.

I'm in control of nothing these days. Maybe I never was. But when I was in New York, it at least felt like I was living my own life.

I should have known that I always belonged to Kincaid Enterprises.

That I'd have to give the company my pound of flesh. I'm sure I was naïve. But also, in some ways, it feels like I'm giving more than any of my brothers. I'm giving up my life, a chance for love, my entire future.

My eyes close, blocking out the bright sun and lush green of the island. Maybe I'll run away. Disappear.

The jarring sound of my phone ringing interrupts my thoughts.

I open my eyes to see Luke's name flashing on the screen. I wince. I've been avoiding him, and I know it.

I love Luke. He's my cousin who is really like a brother. We grew up in the same house. He gave me noogies and beat up the kid who stole my lunch money in fourth grade.

But Luke and Mason are about to kill each other and if Luke understood how much pressure Mason was putting on me, Luke and Mason's relationship would explode, never to be repaired.

I press the screen. "Hello?"

"Hey, Bug," Luke chuckles at his nickname for me. "How's Hawaii?"

"Roman told you?"

"He did. Just like he told me you got engaged."

I nip at my lip. Roman is my youngest brother. Both Roman and I lived with Luke and Luke's mom when my parents died. Even though Roman is my real brother, Luke reads me way better. Of all my male relatives, I'm the closest to him. Which is why, I've been avoiding him. He'll see right through me. "Sorry, Luke. It's been crazy."

"Funny," he rumbles into the phone. "But I can tell that it's not crazy fun."

Shit. Even through the phone, he knows. "It's not that. I was up all night with Cici and Maggie and they kept giving me champagne. I'm just…"

"You? Hungover?" He sounds even more worried.

"Something like that."

"We're going to chat about that one later…" He clears his throat. "When do I get to meet this man who is marrying my best girl?"

"We both know that Kate is your best girl."

"No. Kate is my woman."

That's Luke. Black and white. "I'm a woman too, Lukey."

Luke pauses for a second, tension filling the line, before he says. "I know, Bug. But that doesn't mean that I'm not still looking out for you. I want to meet this man you're marrying."

I shake my head. "Soon. Promise."

"Bug." He says, almost sounding like he might plead. "I love you."

"I love you too," I say, my throat almost feeling raw. The words well up. I could tell Luke everything. Beg for his help. He'd hide me in his very big shadow, he'd get rid of Preston, and he'd force Mason to make other plans without me.

But then… I really would be a little girl. Luke and Mason would never recover and me, I'd be the domino that caused an empire to fall.

"You mean it?"

"With all my heart."

"Then how come we don't talk? How come I haven't met this guy?"

I nip at my lip. Luke isn't taking no for an answer. "You will. I'm seeing his parents tonight. Once that happens…"

"Tonight? Aren't you in Hawaii?" Luke's voice gets harder with every word.

I sink down lower in my seat. "Flying back to Vegas today."

"Is Mason going to be with you when you see them?" Luke thinks he's not as smart as the other Kincaids. But he's sniffing me out like a detective.

"I think so."

"At the charity event?"

"You know about the event?"

"It's Roman and Maddie's event, of course I know. All of Vegas is going to be there. Including Mason."

How did I forget that? I'm falling apart. "Maybe?"

That's when another call comes through. Roman. What's happening? It's like all my brothers have put me in the center of the circle. Roman is the savviest of all my brothers. "Luke, Roman's calling. I'm going to add him in." I could use the buffer to deflect Luke's attention.

"Hey, Bella," Roman says in his smooth baritone. "How are you, beautiful?"

"Sorry, Roman," Luke cuts him off. "Bug and I are in the middle of a discussion. And I won't be distracted. Your fiancé hasn't told you where you're meeting his parents?"

I'm not falling into any Luke traps. "Technically, I met them once already, back in New York, before we were engaged."

I don' t think they remember me. They treated me like I was the flavor of the month, Preston's mother calling me three different names in the five minutes we chatted.

"Answer my question," Luke rumbles.

"Luke," Roman cuts in. "Go easy."

That's the problem with having a family full of successful billionaires. He isn't letting it go. "Preston and I haven't had a chance…"

"I'm going to the event tonight."

"Luke." I plead. This night is going to be stressful enough without adding tension between Luke and Mason. My breath is coming out in short huffs. The driver eyes me in the rearview, clearly aware that I'm distressed.

I can feel the walls closing in as I turn my face to look out the window. But it's no use. My vision blurs and my skin starts to tingle.

"Bug," Luke begins, hearing my breaths. "Bella," his voice gentles. "I promise I won't speak a word to Mason… tonight."

I'm absolutely certain that Luke intends to have that discussion in the future. But if I can stretch the problems out to one at a time... "Promise?"

"Promise."

"Luke," I breathe into the phone. "Please. I can't be the reason you and Mason blow apart. Don't take up the fight. I'll be fine. I've got this."

"I don't know about that," Roman grumps.

"Hmm," Luke says at the same time. I look up to realize we're pulling into the private airstrip where the Kincaid plane awaits. "Mason can railroad the strongest man. I won't let him hurt another woman in our family."

"Another woman?" I ask, my anxiety forgotten with this new piece of information. Now we're getting somewhere interesting.

But Luke is way savvier than I am. "I'll see you tonight, okay?" he deflects.

"Tell me you're bringing Kate at least."

"Of course, I am," he rumbles. "And if it's easier to talk to her, you can tell her what's going on so she can tell me."

I promise nothing. "See you tonight."

"Glad you're going to be there, Bella," Roman says. "Maddie and I appreciate the support."

"I wouldn't miss it." But my hand comes to my forehead. This night is going to be a disaster.

CHAPTER FOUR

Arabella

My hand slides down the sleek black gown in which I'm now draped. Mason had me picked up at the airport and taken straight to a salon.

I should have travelled in my pajamas.

I spent three hours being waxed, styled, and dressed to the hilt. Now I stand next to Preston as a sea of guests pay their respects to our family.

Roman and his wife Maddie started a nonprofit division within Kincaid Enterprises. They service animals who are negatively impacted by the cityscape of Vegas. It's great press for Mason and a true calling for Maddie.

And the reason Roman is still part of the company.

Preston and I have barely spoken, me arriving just before the event began. He stands next to me now, not making eye contact as he shakes hands with the line of guests.

Roman is on my other side, holding Maddie's arm. Maddie is vision impaired so Roman spends most of these events at his wife's side. Not that he'd be anywhere else, even if she didn't need his help.

A bit of jealousy snakes down my spine. Deep in my gut, I know I want a husband like that. One who can't be parted from me. My brother is a great husband.

But that doesn't stop me from whispering in Roman's ear. "You told on me to Luke."

Roman gives me a small smile. "Telling him you're engaged is not tattling. Besides, you should have told him already. How was I supposed to know he didn't know?"

I wrinkle my nose. He isn't wrong. "Luke doesn't understand."

"I don't understand." Then Roman leans closer. "Tell me the truth, Arabella. Do you love him?" He glares around me to Preston.

I give my head a shake. Roman using my full name sparks a memory from last night. Right as I was falling asleep, Gris called me Arabella. How did he…

But Mason is walking up to us, a handsome older couple trailing behind him. Preston's parents. My stomach drops at the sour look on their faces. I ignore it and them, turning to Roman. "You tell me what happened between you, Luke, and Mason and I'll tell you about what's going on with me." I feel Roman stiffen. That's what I thought.

Preston grabs my arm, the first time he's touched me in nearly half an hour, and pulls me toward Mason, ignoring the fact that Roman and I were in the middle of a conversation.

"Mummy," he gushes, stopping in front of his mother. "So glad you're here."

The woman air kisses both Preston's cheeks, then looks at me, her nostrils flaring ever so slightly. "Belle. So good to see you again."

"Bella," Preston corrects, his own lip curling. Is he annoyed with his mother and the fact she can't get my name right or with my name itself? He's mentioned it before, the fact that my name isn't classic.

"Bella, that's right," Mrs. Wingate waves her hand airily like it dispels the mistake. "I can't keep all these newfangled names straight. But yours ought to be an easy one. That's what Mrs. Vieselmeyer named her poodle."

I get her meaning. I don't have one of those old-money names like

Evelyn, or Vivian, or Madeline. My name is literally for the dogs. "It's no problem, Mrs. Wingate, wonderful to see you again."

"And you," she says, but her gaze is already sliding away, down the line of my family. "We'll have to carve out a bit of time to discuss the particulars of the wedding tomorrow. I have some ideas. Breakfast?"

"Lovely." I expected nothing less. Mason has hired wedding planners who are already hard at work planning the Colorado ceremony and reception. I didn't want the wedding in Vegas, Mason didn't want to go to New York. Preston surely would have pressed for the East Coast, but he doesn't dare anger my brother.

Who, speaking of, is giving Mrs. Wingate a very skeptical glare. Gangster or not, Mason is used to getting his way. And as the person funding this wedding, I expect he will again.

Mason is allowing Preston a seat on the board of Kincaid Enterprises and control of my shares. I don't want them. I don't want the business. But it feels strange that Preston will make decisions on my behalf. That my own finances will be his to control. The man who can't even pick up the phone to call me.

I was so stupid to rush into this. To think that the man who'd started to pull away wanted me and not my money. No wonder my brothers are worried. I've been completely sheltered and now I'm making stupid decisions.

"How was your flight?" I ask, but Mrs. Wingate doesn't answer. Her gaze doesn't even flicker to me, her attention held by someone entering the ballroom.

To my right, a man I don't recognize approaches Mason. "Mr. Kincaid, might I borrow you for a moment?"

Mason nods, then looks down at me. "I'll be right back," he rumbles, touching my arm before he strides away.

I watch him for a second, not really wanting to be alone with the Wingates, before I turn to see who the Wingates are watching with such intent.

The crowd parts, a hush falling in a way that sharpens my attention.

All heads turn, mine included, to watch the five men who are entering the ballroom. But I can only stare a at the man in center. My lungs tighten, my breath trapped, as I go numb. Because it's Gris. I don't even know his last name, but I'd recognize him anywhere. And he's here.

What? How? Why? I sway on my feet, reaching for Preston. My hand clamps down on his arm. "Preston," I whisper, my desperation making my voice strained.

He doesn't hear me, doesn't respond. His eyes are on Gris as well. "They're here."

"Who?" I asked, my head swimming.

Preston's fingers bite into my skin then. "The Smiths, of course. All five of them." He's hissing in my ear now. "I can't believe you don't know them. They've worked with your brother in the past. Not any longer, of course."

Of course? What have I missed? Is this something I should have known? But I don't get to ask.

"It's only the one they call Gris that I'm interested in meeting," Mrs. Wingate breathes out, sounding like a sorority girl instead a matron. "Lord Griswold is second in line for the dukedom."

Mr. Wingate gives an appreciative chuckle. "We'll have to invite them for dinner. Friends like that are rare to find and very beneficial to collect..."

I stop listening as I watch Mrs. Wingate step forward, practically waving Gris over. This cannot be happening...

Gris sees her and adjusts course, the other men following. I feel the blood drain from my face as I pray for the floor to swallow me.

But this ballroom is Kincaid built and rock solid. Gris's long strides eat the ground between us and them, stopping to speak with the Wingates before his eyes find me.

His gaze dips down, noting Preston's hand on my arm, before they rise up to meet mine again. "You must be Arabella Kincaid."

The air rushes from my lungs. "Lord Griswold."

"Just Gris," he returns. "It's a pleasure to meet you, Arabella. Give Mason my regards." And then he's gone, leaving me feeling like my bones are about to melt.

"Preston," I say again, needing a moment away.

"What?" he snaps, grimacing down at me.

"Could we get a glass of water please?"

"Now?"

I nod weakly as he wraps an arm around me and pulls me toward our table.

"The conference room," I whisper. "I just need a moment."

"Christ, Arabella," he grinds through his teeth. "What is wrong with you?"

Preston is handsome enough. But I can't help noticing he's got a weak chin and thin shoulders as he steers me toward one of the empty side conference rooms off the main ballroom. "Why did you have to pick now to make such a display?"

"It's just water."

"We had to leave in the middle of introductions. The Smiths are the sort of friends my parents have always wanted."

Gross. "They had already moved on," I snap back, tired of these conversations.

"The evening has barely started, and the networking tonight is important."

He's not wrong there, and I have a moment of regret. I need to step away because I made the worst sort of mistake. I shouldn't be yelling at him. "I'm sorry, Preston. I had a late night last night."

"That's your fault." His grip only tightens.

I look at him, my brows scrunching. He's been so irritated with me of late. It's unrelenting. "Honestly, I could have used a bit more notice this was all happening."

"You'll have to get used to last-minute social engagements. They're part of my world and your new role at Kincaid."

That irritates me. I know all about my family's business. I don't need him to explain it. "And you'll have to get used to calling your future wife and giving her basic updates. Why did my brother have to be the one to tell me your parents were coming?"

He stops, his hand biting into my skin, hard enough to make me wince. "I've been busy learning your fucking job."

I stumble back. He's never talked to me like that before. My eyes mist with tears and I just know. I can't do this.

I look away, blinking back the moisture. The words clog in my throat as I clear it. But I just… I can't. "Preston… I think this is a mis—"

"Shit, Bella, I'm sorry." His tone is completely different as he pulls me into his arms, his nose dropping in my hair. "I didn't mean that, baby. The pressure is getting to me."

I nod, agreeing, because as much as I'd like this over, this is not a conversation for the middle of the ballroom at my brother's benefit. "Go back to the party. I'll get water, and I'll join you and your parents momentarily."

"Sounds good, sweetheart." He gives my forehead a chaste kiss.

He hasn't tried any more than that in months.

In fact, he immediately stopped the sexual pursuit when he asked me to marry him. I thought he was being a gentleman at first, but now…

I don't care. The thought of being in bed with him the way I was with Gris is revolting. Which is so telling.

But still, I have no idea what changed his behavior toward me all those months ago. Maybe it doesn't matter.

He leaves me there, standing by the conference room, as he returns to his parents. I don't watch him go, relief making me feel lighter. I just need a minute to myself.

I slip through the door into the empty room, relieved there is a container of water and glasses on a table by the far wall.

I cross, and with a shaking hand, pour myself a glass. Bringing it to my lips, I let the cold water slide down my throat, cooling my heating body.

What are the chances that the man I fooled around with in Hawaii is here tonight in Vegas? That he's an associate, or former associate, of Mason's?

It's beyond crazy. A million to one…

"Arabella."

I gasp, the glass slipping from my fingers and shattering into a million pieces at my feet, as I spin to find Gris standing in the doorway. "How do you know my name?"

Is that the right question to start with? Probably not.

He cocks his head, staring at me. "You told me."

"No. I didn't."

"Lying to me, Bella?" he saunters closer.

Water is puddling around my shoes. "Everyone calls me Bella. I didn't lie." I shake my head, never taking my eyes off him. This time, I sense the danger.

He keeps moving toward me and my nipples tighten. Even now, that danger is laced with attraction. No weak jaw or small shoulders here. Gris is everything I remember and, in the bright light of the conference room, he's better. I swallow down my fears. "You, however..."

He stops a few feet away, quirking a brow. "I didn't lie."

"Was it a coincidence we met in Hawaii?"

"No."

My hand flutters to cover my mouth, fear pulsing through me. "What was it then? Our meeting?"

He shakes his head. "Not the detail you want to get hung up on."

"What detail should I... get hung up on?"

"I started as a partner to Mason before he royally fucked me on the tunnel he's built under Vegas."

No. I feel my head spin as spots show behind my eyes and I reach for the table.

I should have understood the moment Preston mentioned that Mason and Gris knew each other. Gris was in Hawaii to meet me. I'm his instrument of revenge.

The woman who fell willingly into his bed.

The woman on whom the hopes and dreams of Kincaid Enterprises is resting had a tryst with the enemy.

I'm the worst kind of fool and I deserve whatever's coming. I keep myself standing by sheer force of will. Now is no time to be a swooning female. "I think you should leave."

"But I just got here."

"Please leave." My chin notches.

He looks at me, his gaze starting at my sleek updo and over the fitted gown that highlights my tiny waist. "I don't think so."

"I'll scream."

He takes another step closer, his shoe crunching on the broken glass. Before I've even noticed, he's got me in his arms, lifting me out of the puddle. "You won't."

My arms automatically go around his neck. "You don't know that."

"You don't want to draw attention to me, princess. We both know it." He's so close, his mouth inches from mine as those deep, dark, near black eyes stare into my soul.

Even knowing that he's nothing but trouble, I'm throbbing between my legs, and I can feel the full length of his cock pressing into my thighs. It's a cock that I know intimately. How it looks. How he tastes.

"What do you want?"

"We need to talk."

"Now?"

"Tomorrow," he answers. "Lunch. One o'clock. I'll pick you up."

"Pick me up where?"

His lips curve into a half smile. "At your place."

"How do you know where I live?"

"I know all sorts of things about you, Arabella Kincaid." Slowly he sets me down. "And I know you want to know about me too."

His hands are splayed out on my back, his cock growing harder as my body aches with a desire I'm trying desperately to deny.

I'm in the worst kind of trouble.

CHAPTER FIVE

Gris

Arabella Kincaid has made a deal with the devil.

That would be me. I'm the devil.

I watch from across the room as she kisses the cheek of her cousin, Luke Kincaid.

Next to her, that fucking cunt, Preston Wingate, eyes a passing blonde with fake tits and even faker hair.

The blonde catches his eye and giggles. He smiles in return and subtly shifts his cock. What a stupid fucking prick.

He's barely touched his fiancé all evening, which is fine with me. The moment I walked into this room and saw his hand on her arm, I lost my mind for a second.

Which is a big fucking problem.

I am not supposed to feel anything but detached indifference for the Kincaid Princess.

But the plan is already getting fucked. They usually do. Plans rarely go like you think they should. I just didn't expect this.

First, Bella is a true beauty. She's fucking perfect. Rich, silky brown hair, classic features, completely fuckable lips, a ten for a body with long legs and a gorgeous ass. The exact right amount of tits.

And then there was the way she responded to me. I was only supposed to kiss her. Take her out, shower her with wine and roses. Woo her away from her fiancé with a bit of romance. Help her see she was making a mistake, and fucking Mason Kincaid out of his newest piggybank, Preston Wingate.

But the moment I held her in my arms, she went from shy to molten. It was the best non-sex of my fucking life, and I'm a man who has his pick of women.

So yeah. The plan has already been fucked.

But it doesn't change what happens next. Arabella sold her soul to me, and I am about to cash in.

It's just gotten way messier.

My brother Triston leans close, interrupting my intense staring. "Gris."

"Yeah?"

"You're sure you're still good with this?"

"I'm fucking good," I grit back, knowing that my brother can sense my hesitation. Or infatuation.

We're fraternal twins and something about sharing a womb makes him more in tune with my thoughts than any of my other brothers.

On my other side is my brother Rushton, and next to him is Killian. Crazy fucker. On the end is Ryker.

We all look the same. Tall. Broad. Dark hair, darker eyes. Our father is the second son of the Duke of Upgrove, but when his childless older brother passed a year ago, he became the duke and we all became lords.

I couldn't give two shits about the title.

Our eldest brother is still in England, preparing to take over the dukedom. It leaves the rest of us free to replenish the family fortune.

I love the job. And I'm good at it too. Unlike Mason, who has overleveraged himself, I play the percentages and never spend more than I can afford.

My brothers and I pooled our money three years back, bought a casino, doubled our money, bought another. Tripled it again. Made a deal with the Kincaids that we'd help them with some of their dirty laundry if they allowed us to connect our casinos to their underground tunnel. Anyone in on that project will do far more than triple their assets. It will make us billionaires.

The problem?

My last job for the Kincaids was to deliver the Italian princess, Antonia Carcetti, to the care of Jake Kincaid. Fucker fell in love with his kidnapped victim. Now his victim-turned-bride wants revenge on me. I didn't kidnap her. I didn't seduce her. All I did was ask her out on a date I never showed for.

But she can't blame her husband, can she? Instead, she's decided I'm the villain.

Which means, the Kincaids closed access to us. Fuck that. They want a villain... they're going to get one.

And I've only got a little time left.

Once Mason gets over the financial hump of Luke selling his shares, and financing the tunnel, the man will be unstoppable. That's why I need to act now.

I'm getting my rights back and I'm going to use the same trick they did. I'm going to steal a princess. My gaze narrows on Arabella.

Jake Kincaid fucked up his chance when he fell in love, but that won't be me.

"Do we know why that Preston pansy wants to marry her? I mean besides the fact that she's fucking hot?" Killian asks, rubbing a hand over his mouth as he stares at Arabella.

I snatch his hand from his mouth, my teeth gritting. He can keep his eyes to himself. He glares back, not the least bit intimidated.

"Mason is giving him a seat on the board," Triston answers.

I cock my head to the side, delivering a piece of information I've been holding close. "And control of her shares."

"Shares?" Triston asks. "How much?"

"Twenty percent."

"So the man who marries her gets one-fifth of Kincaid enterprises." Triston pivots forward again. If my brothers had known that detail, they would have been fighting to be the man in that hotel room with Arabella. But it was always going to be me.

"The plan is to break up the wedding. Keep Mason from making more powerful allies so that he has to take our deal instead."

"Or you could marry her," Rush clears his throat. "She's easy on the eyes. Wouldn't be that bad."

"We're not the marrying kind," I answer. But even I have to admit the logic is sound.

"Not even to save us fifty million dollars?" Tris asks. "Need me to step in? She might not even know the difference, we look enough alike. I might make an exception to my no-relationship policy for a piece of ass like that. Coupled with the money…"

My jaw clenches as I give him a hard stare. "Twenty percent is not a controlling share. We'd still have to buy our access. And Mason needs the money, or he'll have to sell a substantial amount of stock. That's why he's sold his sister to that complete piece of shit to begin with."

My brothers can't start getting ideas. I've made promises beyond them, ones they don't know about, to get us this far. My gaze slashes across the Kincaid clan, the tension between them palpable.

Did I take advantage of their internal war? Maybe. But that's what those fuckers get for double crossing me over Nia.

"But Preston doesn't have any money."

"Yeah, but he's got a rolodex of associates who do, and Mason just received access to all of them. He's not giving them shares, but a promise to double their investment within a year. It's a great deal if you've got the money."

Now Preston is the type of guy who will marry a woman to replenish his coffers. All while he looks down on her like she's the one who isn't good enough.

And, apparently, Mason is the sort of man who will sacrifice anyone to Kincaid Enterprises. Even his only sister.

My other hand balls into a fist and I tuck them under my arms to hide my irritation. Arabella turns away from her family, her shaking hand swiping across her forehead.

She feels the noose tightening. I know she does.

And I should be triumphant in this moment. Instead, regret pulls at my chest.

I push the feeling away, turning my back to her. "I've seen enough."

"You got the date tomorrow?" Tris asks.

"Yes," I answer before starting toward the door.

I'm walking a fine line here, between Arabella, her brothers, and my family. Lucky for me, I've got the strength and the cunning to pull this off.

Arabella climbed in bed with the devil.

And now, she's going to have to pay with her soul.

CHAPTER SIX

ARABELLA

I NOD along as Mrs. Wingate grills the wedding planners. *Are they sure that's the right shade of ecru?*

Must the tables be so clunky?

Is there any way to mitigate the smell of pine?

It's Colorado. It's going to smell like pine.

Then she hits me with the line she's said five times already, "Are we certain we don't want to have this wedding in New York? Colorado is so… woodsy."

"Mason's choice," I murmur, tossing my brother under the bus. In some ways, this is far more his wedding than it is mine. Except for I'm the one who will be tied to Preston.

Though Mason will be joined with Preston too, I guess. Once the contracts are dry, Preston will be impossible to remove from Kincaid. Then again, Mason is cunning. Has he found a loophole?

Even if he has, that won't change my fate.

I can't marry him. I know it deep in my heart. I'm just not certain how I'm getting out of it.

Still, it feels like some invisible clock is now ticking. Gris is my brother's enemy. We share this big secret. I'm in so much trouble.

Now there is no way to do this without ripping my family even further apart. And damaging Kincaid Enterprises too.

I half listen to Mrs. Wingate as she looks at the dress samples for the bridesmaids. "Red? Really? It's so tacky."

"It's fall in Colorado," I answer, with a furrow to my brow. It was Maggie and Cici's pick, a deep russet red that will match the foliage. But the other bridesmaids agreed that the color suited them as well. With every bridesmaid on board, the decision is not up for debate.

"Really, Ella," Mrs. Wingate waves an airy hand, her tell that she knows she's getting my name wrong. She's doing it on purpose. "You're marrying a New York socialite, not a woodcutter."

"Bella," I say through clenched teeth. I look up at the wedding planner who stares back aghast as I grip the table with both hands, wondering if it's more alarming that my future mother-in-law has questioned my every decision or that she can't get my name right.

Bile rises up on my tongue as I fight back the urge to tell this woman to take her opinions and stuff them.

The Wingate family made money alongside the Vanderbilts at the turn of the century, but the Wingates lost it even faster. Mr. Wingate has made enough in stocks to keep them at the Yacht Club, but Preston, despite being educated at Yale, hasn't accomplished even his father's success.

None of them hold a candle to my brothers in terms of earning potential.

Still, I'm letting Mrs. Wingate get under my skin.

This isn't me. I don't get angry and yell at people. I'm the peacemaker usually.

So why am I fantasizing about tearing out Mrs. Wingate's throat?

And why haven't I done a better job of managing my brothers? Then again, I might have sensed there was no keeping the Kincaid men together. I tried. By agreeing to marry Preston, I was going to help Luke get out, help Mason succeed.

But I've messed everything up.

I lick my lips, drawing in a deep breath. Maybe what I need to do is get Luke and Mason to make up. If Mason doesn't have to buy out Luke's shares, then he doesn't need Preston's friends to invest, and I don't need to get married.

It's an idea that has me tapping my fingers on the table.

"What's that about?" Mrs. Wingate points at my fingers.

I stop drumming. "Just thinking."

"Do it quietly, Annabella, it's unbecoming to think so loudly."

My mouth snaps shut as I hold my tongue, not bothering to correct her.

I glance down at my watch, realizing that my lunch with Gris is in forty-five minutes. Butterflies fill my stomach at the idea of seeing him. Of being alone with him.

At least we'll be in a crowded restaurant. Then again, that's problematic as well. What if someone sees us together?

I shake my head. I'm acting like a guilty person. Which I am.

But if Gris was at the benefit last night, that means he travels in the Kincaid social circle. Who is to say we're not old friends having lunch? For all anyone knows we might have dated in the past or... This line of thought is not helping. I only end up picturing him naked.

It takes Mrs. Wingate another half hour to go over the details the wedding planners have put into place. "Why don't we plan a day trip to Colorado so you can show me the venue?" Mrs. Wingate isn't speaking to me but to the planner.

Karen looks at me, her gaze questioning. With a small shake of my head, I confirm. "I'll speak to Mason about using the helicopter. Tomorrow?"

Karen nods back, and Mrs. Wingate, finally satisfied, bids me a goodbye. My relief is short-lived as I climb into the car, speeding back to my apartment.

I weave in and out of traffic, the heel of my stiletto my pivot point to work the gas, my other working the clutch. I don't get to drive much in New York, it's one of the advantages of being back in Vegas.

I have an apartment in one of my brother's buildings. The building and the apartment are gorgeous. Much bigger and nicer than what I had in New York. Not that I didn't like my little place in the heart of downtown New York, I loved it.

Mason paid for that place too, just like he paid my tuition. Our mother died first, and then our father a year later. That's when my aunt took in Roman and me, but as soon as Mason graduated from college, he started helping her financially as she raised us. And then he paid for both Roman and me to go to school.

In some ways, he's been like a father, and I really appreciate how much burden he's taken on in life. Twenty-two and supporting his siblings. I think my other brothers forget that sometimes. Mason has sacrificed a lot. And there is a part of him that is always reaching for the security that would lighten his burden. I get it, even if they don't.

Which is why all of this is just so hard.

That's my last thought as I pull into the parking garage of my building to find a long black limo waiting to one side.

I slide my MINI Cooper into its usual spot and step out of the car, adjusting my wrap dress a moment before Gris opens his door and steps out of the back of the limo. My pulse jumps to see him, and I try to tamp down my reaction.

Today, I can't be some wilting flower, and I can't let this attraction override my logic.

He approaches, the masculine sway of his body making my mouth go dry as all my thoughts evaporate.

He's just so…

"You're late."

I don't answer. What do I say…. I was wedding planning with my future mother-in-law. This is the man I did all manner of dirty things with the night before last. Either he thinks I'm the most two-faced person on the planet, or he has some inkling I don't want this marriage.

Both of which are true.

"I'm late for a meeting you have blackmailed me to attend?"

He stops just in front of me, one side of his mouth quirking up before he reaches out a hand. "Shall we?"

I give a stiff nod. Today is about correcting some mistakes.

He takes my fingers and fits them into the crook of his arm, my pulse jumps at the light touch of his fingers and the feel of his muscles under my palm.

Reaching the car, he opens the door, helping me inside. It's the sort of limo that could easily seat ten.

There is a table fully set in one corner with a whole luncheon. I blink in surprise. "We're eating here?"

He slides onto the bench seat next to me. "Our conversation requires a certain level of privacy."

All my muscles tense, a weight settling in the pit of my stomach, any notion of eating gone. "Why?"

His arm wraps around the back of the seat. "Like you don't know."

My heart is hammering in my chest, my eyes wide as they meet his.

"We find ourselves in a rather compromising situation."

I swallow down a lump. "A situation you manufactured."

"Did I? You could have walked out of that room. You're the one who decided to cheat. Not me."

I feel the color drain from my face. "You're right. I did." My voice is a hoarse whisper.

"You're the one who screamed my name."

I might hate him. My hand comes to my stomach as it rolls. "What do you want, Gris?"

Between my breakfast with Mrs. Wingate and now this, my brain fritzes with static, my head spinning.

He leans closer and I catch his fresh woodsy scent. Even as he's the one who's torturing me in this moment, I want to curl into that smell, the strength of his body. It's so crazy, it only makes my head spin more.

"I want…" He leans even closer, overwhelming my senses. "For you to break it off with your fiancé."

I stare at him for a beat, then two, as I try to process those words. He wants me to end things with Preston? "Why?"

"Because, little princess, I can't have your brother making more powerful friends."

He did all those things in the hotel room to get at Mason. I really am just the instrument of his revenge.

It makes me sick to think of how I responded to him. What I let him do to me. How I let him use me and now he's going to hurt my family.

The bile in my throat rises and I know I'm going to be sick.

CHAPTER SEVEN

Gris

Arabella has gone deathly pale, and I fight my own instinct to pull her close. Comfort her.

This is not like me.

I don't get all gooey for women, I don't have a soft center.

But I've never been closer to taking back my words as her frantic and wild eyes search the limousine.

And then she makes a dive for the empty champagne bucket, grabbing it and hugging it to her chest as she tips her head down and heaves into the bucket.

"Fuck," I growl out, reaching out to gather up the silky strands of her hair to hold them back.

I've had this hair in my hand before, gathered up in my fist as I watched that stunning mouth wrap around my cock. What she lacked in skill, she more than made up for in enthusiasm. It was the best blowjob of my entire life. I can't even imagine what she'd be like with some practice.

My other hand comes to her forehead, helping to hold the weight of her head as she empties her stomach.

I know she understands the full measure of what's happening. What she did with me in that hotel room is a secret capable of taking Kincaid Enterprises and blowing it to the four corners of the world.

It's also possible that it destroys my family along with it. I've been playing every side and that's a gamble that could backfire.

I hate that I'm the man holding the guillotine over her head. I feel deep in my gut that I should be protecting her.

But that's not the play here.

Wrongs need to be righted. Futures made and others destroyed.

That thought steals my spine as she falls limply back on the seat. I take the bucket from her hand, opening the limo door, and step out. Knocking on the driver's door, I hand him the bucket. "Get rid of this."

He's professional enough not to ask, but I see his brows rise as he takes the bucket. I climb back in to find Arabella exactly where I left her.

"You want me to end my engagement?" she asks, tossing a hand over her eyes as she leans back on the seat. She looks like she might be sick again.

"That's right." I sit next to her, brushing her hair back from her forehead. She's too limp to resist as her lip trembles, her hands shaking right along with it. Fuck.

"And if I don't?"

I appreciate that she asked. It makes it easier. "I'll do it for you."

She turns to me then, her face so pale, her eyes are like saucers. "You'll do it for me?"

"I'll start with Mason and then Preston and then—" She bats my hand away from her forehead.

"Let me out." She pushes up from her seat, nearly falls and stumbles toward the door.

I easily catch her, pulling her into my lap. At this rate, she's going to plant face first into the cement.

But she reacts like a wild cat, twisting and scratching in my arms.

"Bella," I whisper, calmly holding her to keep her from hurting me or herself. "Stop."

"Let me go," she cries, a broken sob erupting from her lips. My insides twist again. This is so much more difficult than I imagined.

"I would never hurt you."

"You are hurting me," she hurtles back. "Hurting my whole family."

"I'm not," I hug her tightly to my chest, the fight ebbing out of her. "We both know I'm doing you a favor. Marriage to Preston would be a prison."

She goes from wildcat to completely still in my arms. "How do you know that?"

I can't help myself, I brush a kiss across her forehead, damp with her sweat. She's laying across my lap now and I slide my free hand into her hair, cradling the back of her head.

It's a dangerous game I'm playing, holding her like this. I cannot allow any more emotion into this equation. But I can't quiet resist softening the blow I'm delivering.

I'm well aware she's weakened my position already. Beautiful, caring, delicate. She's been caught between prowling tigers. She messed around with me in Hawaii because she's desperate, confused, and alone. She's in a trap and lashing out. Looking for comfort and possibly escape.

And I just made that trap tighter.

I rest my cheek on her forehead. "I'll give you a week."

"A week to end my engagement?" Her eyes are closed. They flutter open, meeting mine and that's when I see it. The flecks of gray that color them. The steel that's under the warm brown.

She sits up, pulls out her phone, and hits a button. She presses another and I hear the ring, a second before Preston's pansy voice sounds through the speakers. "I'm in the middle of a meeting, Bella. What do you want?"

She hesitates for a moment before she draws in a breath. "I need to speak with you about—"

"Later." And then he hangs up the phone. I want to punch him in the face. Then again, I'm no better.

For a second, she stares down at it, before she reaches for her finger and pulls the ring off, closing her fingers around it.

Then she looks at me. Our eyes meet and I straighten, sensing what's coming...

"I'll break it off tonight." There is no more tremble in her voice. "But just to be clear, I never want to see you again."

Then she opens the door to the limo and steps out. She doesn't even close the door.

I hear the tap of her heels as she walks away.

Fuck.

Maybe I should have listened to Triston. Proposed marriage, offered her some deal of her own. I could have been her hero.

Now, I'm just another villain. And Arabella Kincaid, I can add her to the list of women who hate my guts.

CHAPTER EIGHT

ARABELLA

I GIVE myself the afternoon to cry.

At five, having barely eaten breakfast, and then having thrown it up in a bucket, I order from my favorite Thai place.

I didn't have lunch either and I know I'm going to need fortification before I call Mason.

Preston hasn't called me back.

I fire off a text to Luke, asking him to meet me for drinks. He responds instantly naming a time and place. I accept with a small smile. I've got to start mending my family somewhere.

Raw and in my sweats, I eat my dinner, trying to keep my stomach from revolting again. I'm not looking forward to the next conversation I need to have.

Tossing the containers out, I pick up my phone and call Preston again. It's after six, he should be between the office and before his dinner, he likes to eat late.

But he doesn't pick up.

I sigh out my frustration. I just want this call over with. Do I go to his hotel? Camp out until he comes through the lobby?

He's staying under the Kincaid name. I might even be able to get a key to his room…

But I don't have to do any of those things as my phone rings, Preston's name popping up.

"Hey," I say, already sounding breathless as I pick up the phone.

"Hey," he replies back, clearly distracted. "Are you dressed?"

I blink down at the phone. What kind of question is that? "I'm not naked, if that's what you're asking."

"Jesus, Bella." As usual, he sounds irritated. "For dinner. Are you dressed for dinner?"

I'm so sick of this. Sick of him and the constant implication that I'm not enough. That I've messed things up. "Preston, why would I be dressed for dinner?"

"Because…" he snaps back. "We're dining with your brother and my parents tonight."

My mouth drops open. "You might be, but I'm not."

"I told you—"

"You told me nothing, as usual."

"Last-minute invitations are part of the bargain."

"Whose bargain? Which bargain?" I feel my anger rising like the tide. "How long have you known about this dinner that you didn't bother to tell me about? Stop acting like it's always my fault and never yours."

"I told you—"

"I'm tired of this, Preston. I'm not going out to dinner tonight." I glare at my phone, no part of me wanting to back down.

"Get fucking dressed," he grits into the phone. "I'll be there in twenty minutes."

"No."

"You get dressed, or so help me God, the wedding is off."

Is he breaking it off with me? Is this actually happening? "Fine by me. The wedding is off. Goodbye, Preston." And then I hang up. There. It's done. And honestly, it was far easier than I thought.

A light giddiness steals through me. I'm free.

I know it's going to get ugly, but in this moment, relief is the only emotion I feel, grinning at the bay window in my living room.

I draw in a ragged breath and look down at my phone. I'll need to call Mason. My whole plan for remaining engaged was to first get Luke and Mason to make up. Then I could end things without worry of Mason, Luke, or Kincaid Enterprises suffering.

If I'm going to get this right, though, I need more information.

Biting my lip, I look down at my phone. Roman, Luke, and I grew up together. Mason has been like a father.

But I have one other brother, the second oldest, Leo.

Leo and I aren't close.

When my father died, Leo took the first bus to crazy town. Muscled and unhinged, my other brothers have kept me from Leo.

But he met a woman, married, and has a baby on the way, and honestly, he's like a completely different man.

With that in mind, I hit the button and place the call. Leo's phone rings twice before he picks up.

"Ari? Is that you?"

"Hey, Leo," I say, scuffing one of my feet on the floor. "It's been a while."

"I saw you at the benefit two nights ago." I can hear a crowd in the background. Leo runs our clubs. His wife, Kim, was one of his dancers. He must be at one of them now.

"Right. I forgot."

"You were busy looking miserable."

"Did I?" I wince. "Shit."

"No swearing," he admonishes, sounding more like an older brother than I have ever heard him.

"Sorry."

"You gonna tell me why you're calling. Something wrong?"

"I..." I take a big breath. "I just broke it off with Preston."

"Thank God. What a fucking twat that guy is. Need me to beat the shit out of him?"

I start to giggle but it turns in a full-blown chortle that has me bent over in glee. "Not yet. But I'll let you know," I finally push out. I've never loved Leo more.

"Ari," he says, using his own nickname for me. "I know I haven't been a very good brother."

"It's all right, Leo. I've got plenty of male influence. If you'd joined in, I wouldn't have gone to school in New York, I would have had to go as far as France or maybe even Japan."

It's his turn to laugh. "Right."

"I did want to ask you something, though." I draw in a deep breath. "Mason isn't going to be happy when he finds out about me and Preston."

"Fuck. Yeah. If you're calling because you need me to stand between you and our bossiest brother, you got it sister. I never miss a chance to kick Mason's ass."

Leo and Mason fight like cats and dogs. But somehow, they manage to stay together. Maybe it's because Leo just calls Mason out on his shit and then they punch each other. "I might have to take you up on that."

"Good."

"But that isn't why I called."

"No?"

"I… um… I'm wondering what happened between Roman, Luke, and Mason."

Leo lets out a long breath. "Roman and Luke didn't tell you?"

"No. They've been super mum."

Leo is quiet for a second and I think he's not going to tell me. "Basically, Mason was being his controlling self. He didn't tell Roman that Luke was alive when Luke disappeared because he wanted Roman to keep up with the tunnel project. And then, he manipulated Luke into almost ruining Kate's career."

I stare at the phone. "Mason loves us. Why would he do that?"

"Because…" Leo lets out a really long breath. "He wants us to be untouchable. He doesn't want what happened to dad to happen to any of us. But sometimes, he loses the forest through the trees, you know."

Yeah. I get that. He's doing the same thing with me and Preston. Trading my happiness for a new network.

"Thanks for telling me, Leo. That really helps. It explains why Luke is so pissed."

"Yeah. It sure does. But what I want to know is why knowing that helps you?"

"Hmmm," I lick my lips. Leo has been honest, I should be too. "Promise you won't tell?"

"Pinky swear," his deep voice rumbles into the phone.

"I'm going to try and convince Luke not to sell his shares."

"Fuck." Leo gives a low whistle. "Go big or go home."

"I..." I run my fingers over my counter, my nose twitching. "I might need help, Leo."

"Finesse is not my strength, but I'll do what I can."

"Thanks," I whisper, glad that I called him. I like this Leo. I'm about to tell him, when a knock sounds at my door. My brow furrows. I don't get much company.

"What was that?" Leo asks, the protective brother coming out in an instant.

"Bella, open up," Preston calls, banging again. "We need to talk."

"Shit. It's Preston. He's here."

"Need me to come over? I'm only ten minutes away."

"I don't know. Maybe. Can you hang on for a second?" I walk over to the front door, peering out into the hall through the peephole. I see Preston, looking furious. Behind him is Mason. I bring the phone to my ear. "You don't need to come. Preston brought Mason."

"The cavalry?"

"Something like that."

Leo lets out a heavy sigh, like he's feeling bad for me. "Trying to convince you to give the engagement another go?"

"I imagine so," I answer in no rush to answer the door.

"Bella, open the door." Preston bangs again. "We're already late."

"Open the door and then give the twat the phone," Leo rumbles in my ear. "I've got a few things to say to him."

I slide the lock over and then twist the knob.

"What took you so long?" Preston is almost purple, his hands clenched at his side.

I don't answer as I hand him the phone. "Leo wants to talk to you."

Mason glares at me over Preston's shoulder. "Really? Leo?"

I notch my chin. "Preston brought reinforcements, why can't I?"

"I'm not—"

Through the phone, I can hear Leo spitting and cursing as Preston goes from purple to pale.

I cross my arms. "What do you want then, Mason?"

"Can you please come to dinner tonight? We can discuss you and Preston later."

Preston hangs up my phone, pressing it back into my hand. "Your brother is—"

I hold up my hand. "I don't need your opinion. Not anymore."

Preston's mouth presses into a firm line. "Can we talk? Please?"

I shake my head and then my gaze meets Mason's. His eyes silently plead. "I'll go to dinner with your parents. I don't want to talk."

Preston gives a curt nod.

I turn and, leaving the door open, head for my room. Time to trade the sweatpants for the heels.

I'm reading in twenty minutes. It would have been sooner, but my eyes are still puffy, so I needed some artful makeup.

No one talks as we take the limo from my apartment to the restaurant. When we enter, it's apparent that we're late.

Preston's parents are seated with three other men I don't recognize. Mason immediately begins handshaking, leaving me with Preston as his mother approaches. "Darling, there is fashionably late and then there is just rude." She shoots me a glare.

"Apologies, Mother. It's my fault. I forgot to add this dinner to the calendar, so Bella didn't know it was happening."

Mrs. Wingate rolls her eyes and my teeth snap together. I am not in the mood for this.

My teeth lock tighter together. At least in a few hours, I'll be meeting Luke. And this time, I'm coming armed with the kind of information that might make this nightmare end.

CHAPTER NINE

Arabella

Three hours later I sit at the bar, a sparkling seltzer water in front of me, waiting for Luke.

He's late and I'm annoyed.

The last few hours have been a lesson in pain, coupled with the hours of crying, I'm tired.

I refuse to watch the door, but it takes all my energy not to glare at it in anticipation.

The bartender has been eyeing me for the last twenty minutes, I know he's working his way up to asking me out.

That last thing I need is another man to manage. I'm full up.

I take a sip of my seltzer and turn away as the bartender tries to make eye contact for the third time in the last minute. But I wish I hadn't. In fact, I'd wish I'd smiled back and flirted shamelessly.

Instead, my gaze collides with the man who is walking through the door.

Gris.

How does he even know I'm here? This time, I know it's not a coincidence. I told him just hours ago that I didn't want to see him again.

I turn back toward the bar, closing my eyes and trying to collect myself.

"You all right?" the bartender asks.

My eyes pop open. "Fine. Thank you."

The bartender eyes Gris as he slides into the chair next to me. I clench the glass of water, needing something to hang onto.

"Princess."

"Asshole."

I see his lips curl into a smile. "I see you're still wearing your ring."

I turn toward him, tossing him a healthy glare. "What are you doing here?"

"I need to speak with you."

"Well, I don't need to speak with you. You should leave."

"I'm not leaving until I've said—"

"I'm done listening to you. I heard what you had to say already." I'd leave, but Luke should be here any second. I pick up my phone and call his number.

"If you're calling Luke, don't bother. He isn't coming."

The phone slides away from my ear as I stare at Gris. How would he know Luke's plans. By slow degrees, the truth sinks in. "I'm going to kill him."

"Hey, babe," the bartender leans over the bar. "You good? You sure you don't need some help?"

Calmly, I set my phone down on the bar and I draw in a deep breath. "I don't need help. Like I said. I'm fine." I'm not fine. Luke, the brother I love most in this world, is part of this scheme against me. What in the world is happening?

"Luke sent you tonight, didn't he?"

Gris doesn't answer, but his grimace tells me all I need to know.

Slipping from the stool, I start for the door. I won't cry. I'm not going to yell. Yet.

Gris falls in step behind me as I dial my phone again. Luke doesn't pick up. I charge out of the bar, the cooler night air filling my lungs as my call goes to voicemail.

I've been a victim this whole time.

It's my fault. I take responsibility. I accepted Preston. I let Mason make all these plans. I trusted Luke when I shouldn't have. Okay, that last one was not my fault.

I get his voicemail. "Luke Kincaid, you call me back in the next five minutes or I will never speak to you again." I hang up.

Gris is behind me, I can feel him. Spinning, I give his chest a hard push. These emotions I can't control are welling up inside me. What is happening? Mason is trapping me, Luke is double-crossing me. No wonder all the Kincaid men want to kill each other. "Go away, Gris."

"We're not done."

"We're done." And then I pull up the Uber app on my phone, tears making it difficult to read.

Frustrated and just wanting to escape, I spin blindly away, stepping out into the crosswalk. I barely see the flash of headlights before sick dread freezes my limbs.

I see the car, feel it baring down on me, but I just...

Strong hands yank me back and suddenly I'm against Gris's hard chest as the car whizzes by, the wind blowing my hair across my back. I grip his biceps, my held tilting back to look up into the dark depths of his eyes. "Gris?"

He wraps his arms tighter around me, his nose dropping into my hair. "You're all right. I've got you."

I blink up at him twice, just trying to understand. I'm exhausted, physically and emotionally, and I can feel my body sinking.

His arms around me tighten. "I'm going to take you home."

"Yes, please." I know I told him I never wanted to see him again. That I just stormed out of the bar. But what just happened has melted away the last of my fight. I've got no more today. If anything, I just want to sink into his strength.

I know all he's done. Then again, I'm not exactly a pillar of virtue over here. I've done a bunch wrong, but it's time to learn from my mistakes. Which means, I shouldn't give too much away to this man.

He's using me to get revenge on Mason. He'll use any information I give him to his advantage. But right this second, I don't need to talk…

I'm off my feet and in his arms. It's so like that night in Hawaii, the way he feels, I wish for a moment I could be back there.

Back to the feel of his skin before I knew everything else.

My phone rings, but my face is buried in Gris's shoulder, and I barely register the sound.

He stops, still holding me, he whispers. "Take out your phone, luv." It's still gripped tightly in my hand. He sets me down long enough so that I can pull my arm between us, looking down at the phone.

My eyes are blurry, but I can still read Luke's name.

Right. I told him to call me back. I fumble to push the button. "Luke?"

"Bug…"

His stupid pet name for me fills my mouth with acid. I hang up again. I just don't want to hear anything else in this moment. I'm done listening.

Still holding me, Gris takes the phone out of my hand and calls Luke back. He lifts me up again, with one arm and, he starts carrying me down the street. Even though my phone is pressed to the ear that I'm not resting against. I can still hear everything.

"What's wrong, Arabella?" Luke asks.

"It's me," Gris answers.

"Where is Arabella?" Luke demands.

"I've got her. I'm taking her home."

"What the hell happened tonight? You said you needed to talk with her. Why is she so upset?"

I lift my head, my brow scrunching.

Luke does not sound like he's betrayed me. Then again, Luke's an idiot.

"Arabella wasn't looking where she was going and stepped out in front of a car."

"Are you fucking kidding me?" Luke spits into the phone.

"She's all right. I'm taking her home."

"I take it, since you called me from her phone, that she knows you and I are—"

"She knows the basics. I'll explain the rest to her tomorrow. Right now, I think she needs some sleep."

We reach his car, and he opens the passenger door, practically pouring me into the bucket seat.

I distantly note the smell of rich leather before he's around to the driver's side, starting the car and taking off into Las Vegas traffic.

A million questions swirl in my head. But the one that pops out of my mouth, "How'd you learn to drive on the other side of the road?"

He chuckles. "Took a bit of time."

"Will you be the duke someday?"

"Unlikely, but possible."

I let out a long breath. "How many spots are you away from being an actual king?"

"Fourteen."

I guess I don't want to discuss anything of consequence. My heart is aching. And I don't want to tell Gris anything I'll regret. So instead, I keep asking about his life away from Las Vegas. "Do you like the weather in England?"

"It's dreadful. Then again, all this sun is almost oppressively happy."

I smile. "I liked New York. Summer, winter, everything in between. It snowed at Christmas sometimes."

I'm curled into the seat, my eyes closed. His finger brushes over my cheek. "I like New York too. I like Boston even better."

"Oh yeah, why's that?"

"I don't know. It's older. Smaller. Homier."

I feel myself unwind. It's so nice to have a regular conversation. "I'll go someday. When this is all over. I mean, if I can afford it."

"Afford it?"

I shake my head. "Mason's cutting me off at some point, I'm sure. I may never trust Luke again. Maybe Roman will help me out… or Leo. Then again, I'm not sure I want to ask. I've been a burden enough."

He's silent as I kick off my heels and draw my knees up. I'm in a dress, curled in his seat like a small child. And maybe it's childish, but I have this feeling like I just want out of this whole life. Of this mess. Escape.

I'm in the vortex of a tornado, and one wrong misstep, I'm going to be drawn in, flung to some unknown place, likely in a broken heap.

"I seriously doubt your family finds you to be a burden, Bella. They all love you."

"I am a burden." I open my eyes, but I turn away from him to look out the window. I've only ever sucked resources, I've never been an asset. "The one time I brought something of value, Preston's contacts, I messed it all up."

And that's the truth.

Gris is silent for a minute. Two. It goes on so long, I get lost in my own thoughts. The hum of the engine and the passing city.

But as we reach the garage of my building, he finally speaks, "Luke sent me to Hawaii to save you."

CHAPTER TEN

Arabella

"Save me? You?" I snort, my eyes still closed. "You are the last man who should be unleashed on an unsuspecting female."

"Too true. Don't be mad at him, though. His intentions were to send more of a Prince Charming, I think. Convince you that you might find someone besides Preston when you couldn't deny your attraction to me."

"I don't believe that Luke sent you to be a Prince Charming without supervision."

"You weren't speaking to him, he was worried." I open my eyes in time to catch Gris's wince. "And I did it once before. With Nia Kincaid."

That one makes me sit up. "You're kidding me."

"I was the perfect gentleman," he lifts a hand from the shifter and holds his palm up like he's swearing an oath. "With her."

"You? And Nia?" It's like peeling an onion, these stories about my family. How do I not know any of this?

He shakes his head. "I pretended to be interested in her and then when she came out to meet me for a date, Jake intercepted her and brought her out to the desert."

My brow scrunches. "Are you saying that my uncle Jake kidnapped his now-wife?" What the actual hell is happening?

"Yes. I am saying that. And by the way, your brothers were all in on it."

My brothers? I really should have gone off to school in Europe. New York was not far enough.

"But..." he says as he rubs his hand over his thigh, "you're right about Luke expecting me to remain a gentleman. I went to Hawaii with my own agenda."

I grimace as I turn my body and my face straight ahead. He did just save me from getting smacked into a million pieces, but now I'm alive so that he can continue to blackmail me. I shouldn't give him too much credit.

"But Bella..." His voice takes on this note, a softness I haven't heard before. The sound pulls my gaze back to him. "I didn't mean for it to go as far as it did and I..." He tapers off as he parks the car. "I made promises to my family, but I hate that you're hurting."

I frown. "Thanks." But his regret doesn't change anything. It's a nice token, but it isn't real currency.

"I told you the truth about Luke because..." He draws in a deep breath through his nose. "I wanted you to have the power to destroy me too."

My lips part as I stare at him. "What?"

"If Luke found out what we did..." Gris grimaces. "I like Luke. He's the best mate I've had in a long time."

I can't trust that he isn't manipulating me again, but I also can't help going a bit soft inside. He's not just trying to hurt me, he's giving me the power to hurt him too.

I open the car door, and step out into the garage, closing it behind me. Then I start toward the elevator.

With everything I learn, I feel less safe, more vulnerable. I can feel tears welling again, but I push them back, pulling my shoulders straight as I walk toward the elevator. Maybe I'll leave tomorrow. Book a flight to some tropical island and never come back.

Then again, is there anywhere far enough to escape my family?

Their resources are endless, their reach far. Would they let me go?

"Arabella?"

I push the button on the elevator several times, praying for it to open and take me away. I can't even escape Gris.

He steps up next to me, his hand warm and strong at my back. "Let me walk you up."

"I don't want anything from you," I whisper. A lie.

Even now, I want to sink into his arms.

He knows it too. He wraps an arm around me as the elevator opens, guiding me inside.

I don't fight him. I don't have the strength or the desire. But as the door closes, I notch my chin to look at him. "I'm not sure I'm tough enough for this fight, Gris. I've always left that to my brothers. You chose the wrong Kincaid to be your instrument."

His arms come around me, his forehead dropping to mine. "Just lean into me, luv."

I'd snort again, but I'd be the biggest hypocrite, the way my weight sinks into his muscular frame.

I don't tell him that I already ended it with Preston. Don't tell him that I only went to dinner for Mason. I just stand there, letting the warmth of his breath fan my face, his hands spread wide over my back.

"I'm really more of the peacemaker. Or maybe just a coward."

"I don't know. You got pretty tough with Luke."

I smile into his chest. "Mason is going to be furious about all of this if he finds out."

His arms tighten as the elevator opens. "I'll handle Mason if he gets out of hand."

It's a promise I doubt he'll keep, but I still appreciate it. And, honestly, I know Gris isn't my hero. I've always known that.

But maybe, just for tonight, I'd like to pretend.

We walk down the hall and reach my apartment. He takes the key from my hand and opens the door.

I haven't lived here long, but I loved decorating this place.

I took everything I learned in design school and poured it into my new home.

From the drapes to the furniture, it's so me.

Gris swings the door open and flicks on the lights.

I expect him to say goodnight, but with his hand at my back again, he helps me inside and then he closes the door behind him.

CHAPTER ELEVEN

Gris

Arabella scared the shit out of me tonight. I don't scare often, but she rocked me to my core.

She doesn't know it yet, but I'm not going anywhere.

I will beg, borrow, or steal, but I'm staying tonight.

But she doesn't argue as I close the door and click the lock. I can see that the events of the last few days are wearing on her.

She wasn't made for this kind of fight. She's soft, gentle. She's the type of woman who should be protected.

I know it deep down, even though we've only known each other for a few days. And here's the thing about me, I've got strength in spades.

I've always kept a tight rein on my feelings. I don't let them get involved, I don't do soft or fuzzy.

But Arabella is worming her way past my defenses. It started with the way we both lost control that first night.

But now, I see her trying so hard to stand tall when every male around her keeps pushing her down.

It makes me want to knock in their teeth.

My gaze sweeps over her place. It's spectacular.

Her decorating is honestly worthy of the aristocracy.

The textures are perfect, with the silks of the drapes complementing the fabrics of the upholstery.

The chairs and sofa aren't matching sets, but they blend seamlessly. It's the kind of quality that a person can't fake.

I pull Arabella close again. "I love your place."

"Really?" she asks, her voice taking on an air of breathless excitement. "I love it too, but no one else seems to notice."

"Not even Preston? Doesn't his family tout themselves as old money?"

"They did build their fortune at the turn of the century. Railroad money."

"Americans," I mutter into her hair. I feel her soft laugh as she relaxes into me.

"Oh please, the Wingates have us beat by a country mile. My family has had money for five minutes."

"And yet, you have far better taste than any of them." My mother is a duchess. She has taste.

The Wingates are hacks.

"That's the nicest thing anyone has ever said to me." Her arms come around my neck.

I lift her into my arms. It hits me again, how much this woman suits me. Beautiful, talented, sexy, soft in all the ways I need.

I open a few doors, finding her room and carrying her inside.

"You shouldn't be here," she murmurs but she's totally pliant in my arms.

"But I am here and I'm not leaving for a while." I know I'm an asshole. Ordering her around in her own place.

"Gris."

"I'll just hold you. It's been a shit day, and you need some sleep. Let me do this for you."

She lifts her head, giving me a soft smile. "And you think having you in bed with me is going to help me sleep? I don't remember much sleep happening last time."

I chuckle, setting her down on her feet, even as I reach for the zipper in the back of her dress.

I've only ever seen her in a dress or naked. She looks as natural as any aristocrat in heels and the knee-length silk gown fits like it's made for her.

But if I have anything to say about it, I'm keeping her in bed for as long as possible in nothing but my T-shirt.

The dress falls to the floor, pooling around her feet. "Gris." This time, my name has a lot more judgment. She sounds like my favorite primary school teacher. I loved that woman.

My eyes travel down her lacy bra, over the gorgeous indent of her waist, and down to her matching thong.

"I can just hold you, luv, like I promised. But just to be clear… I am available for other services."

"Are we negotiating again?" And then she steps out of the dress, removing one heel and then the other.

She picks up the dress and walks toward the closet, her ass on full display in the thong.

I was already rock hard but watching her walk, I start leaking cum. Jesus.

"Once again, luv, it's for you to make the rules."

"Is that because you have another agenda in mind, my lord?"

Fuck. How did she know the proper address? I don't give a fuck about being a lord, but on her lips, it sounds so good. She disappears into the closet and then comes out again, leaning against the door jamb.

I practically growl as my eyes roam over her. "No agenda other than the fact that I love the way you taste and the way you sound when you cum."

Her breath catches, her body giving a little shiver and I know she's mine tonight. I'm unbuttoning my shirt before she has answered, tossing it in one of the chairs that she's got in a little sitting area under the windows. I kick off my shoes and stride over to where she stands.

I'm going to collect my woman and then I'm going to eat her until she screams.

I see her eyes dilate, her tongue darting out to lick her lips. "I feel like I should run."

"I'd catch you."

"I know." Her hand trembles. "You're going to devour me, aren't you?"

I'm about to say yes, when I catch the double meaning of the words. She's afraid of me.

She should be.

I reach her, my hand snaking out to grab her ass, to pull her into my body. She's got to push up on tiptoes for her arms to come around my neck, her fingers twining into my hair. "Or you could cum so pretty that I can't make myself leave your bed."

One of her perfect brows arches up. "Is that what it takes?"

I don't answer as I reach for her jaw with my other hand, bringing her face to mine as I kiss her long and deep.

She's so fucking pliant in my arms, her body molding to mine, her lips meeting my every touch.

I part hers, and thrust my tongue into her mouth, wanting more of her taste.

I think I really might have meant those words.

This woman could chain me to her pussy.

With a handful of her ass, I pull her even closer until she takes the hint and wraps one of her legs around my hips, opening up her legs so that my cock can nestle against her heat.

I'm still wearing my dress slacks, more precum collecting in my boxer briefs.

I didn't ask her about my orgasm this time. Much as I'd like to cum, I care more about her pleasure tonight.

She deserves something for all the trouble I've caused her.

She's rubbing against me, little cries and moans filling my mouth.

I'd like to make her cum standing right here, but instead, I'm lifting her in my arms again. One hand snakes up to the hooks of her bra and I open that shit one-handed.

The scrap of lace pops off and I take one her perfect tits into my mouth. She arches back, her nipple puckering against my tongue as she tugs my hair.

Fuck, I want to be inside her.

I give her other breast equal attention. I don't play favorites as I lay her down on the bed.

"God, I love your skin," she moans, both her legs locked around my waist now.

"My skin?" I was hoping for muscles. Cock even.

"It feels so good," she moans, her hands sliding down my back. "Warm, rough, masculine."

I stand corrected. I kiss between her breasts and then down her chest. "Yours is like silk, luv. I've never felt softer."

She sighs, her body writhing to meet my every kiss. She smells amazing, like citrus and something floral with the perfume of sex all mixed together.

I reach her belly button, which is adorable, and promptly stick my tongue in it. There isn't a hole of hers that I don't want to explore.

She giggles, tugging at my hair again.

I start to slide lower, ready to taste her. And then, if she'll let me, I'm going to bury myself deep inside her.

She was tight around my finger, around my cock she's going to feel so fucking good.

I kiss over her mound and then slide my shoulders between her thighs. "After I'm done making you scream, I want to be inside you," I rumble before I take a big lick. But she doesn't respond the way I expected.

She stiffens instead, going still.

I lift up my chin as she pushes up onto her elbows, her tits looking absolutely stunning. I can already see a flush climbing up her chest and neck, infusing her skin.

She's got this gorgeous pale skin, which means I can actually see the color climb. "I..."

My brows lift. "Is this because of the engagement?"

"No," she shakes her head, and she sounds sure.

"Because of what I did earlier?"

"Not even that," she says as she bites her lip. "I…" Her little pink tongue darts out to lick her lips. "Gris, I've never…"

A growl climbs up my throat and erupts from my lips. "You're a virgin?"

She's splayed out for me, her pussy spread open like a fucking buffet, just a few inches from my face. I see her cheeks darken even more, turning a bright red. "I'm not a prude."

"I know." I don't want to break eye contact, so I bring the pad of my thumb to her clit and start massaging light circles. We are not stopping this party, we're just slowing it down for a minute.

"In New York I had this security detail, which made dating difficult. It wasn't until after Toni died that I finally had some freedom. That's when I met Preston."

While he's the last guy I want to talk about, I can't believe that he hasn't touched her. What the fuck is wrong with that guy? Then again, his loss is my gain. "No wonder you went out with him. He was the first guy who came along when you finally had some freedom."

"I hadn't thought of that." She looks away… "Anyway, I'm not sure today is the right day for me to… you know…"

I give a quick nod, agreeing, before I dive back into her pussy. She's right. There isn't enough trust yet between us, but I make some promises to myself and silently to her.

I'm going to be the guy. The guy that takes her first. And then, at least for a hot minute, she'll be mine, and only mine.

That thought is way more satisfying than I ever imagined.

Arabella is a goddess, and I eat her pussy like a starving man. It takes almost no time before she's panting my name, her fingers threading into my hair as she pulls me closer, begging for more friction.

Fuck. I might have to move in. I want to do this every night.

I insert a finger inside her, then another, feeling the stretch even as she cries out her pleasure.

I get this overwhelming feeling that I belong in bed with this woman.

I know I'm losing my shit, breaking rules I never break, all because she cries my name in the sweetest fucking voice. I tell myself not to lose my head.

But I'm already weakening. That shit I told her about Luke. It wasn't the smart play.

If I'm not careful, I'm going to ruin everything.

CHAPTER TWELVE

ARABELLA

I FEEL THE ORGASM BUILDING, my nails digging into Gris's scalp. This man can slip past all my defenses, make me forget reason, and turn me to jello in an instant.

I should be remembering that he is a huge part of my current problems.

Instead, I'm mostly fixated on the fact that this is the best I've felt all day.

And I should be taking from him and not giving a damn thing, but I hear myself gush, "I want to suck your cock after."

Which makes him stop.

I cry out, the orgasm so close, the last thing I wanted was for him to stop.

"You want to suck my cock?" His words are a rumbling growl.

Is that weird? How would I know? I feel myself blushing again. "I just… I like it. Your… um… cock is kind of amazing and…"

He's moving up my body before I can even get the words out.

"You like my cock?"

"Is that not something I'm supposed to say?"

Instead of answering, he kisses me, my scent all over his lips and tongue as he shoves it in my mouth.

His cock is now pressing into my drenched folds, sinking just into my entrance.

Did I say I didn't want to have sex with him?

In this moment I want to give him anything. Everything.

All of me. My body any way he wants it. My heart stutters in my chest but I ignore it as he breaks off the kiss and lifts up a few inches, staring down at me. "You can tell me as often as you want, that you like my cock, luv."

I've stopped blushing but I feel my skin heating again. "This… this is just between us, right?" I don't know why, but it feels like I've shared another secret with him. It turns out, I'm wanton. In fact, I'm downright slutty.

"This is completely between us," he answers back, and he sinks just a little deeper inside me. Not enough that it hurts, it's barely the tip, and holy shit, it feels amazing. "You tell me what you like, what you don't, it's only for me, princess. No one else will ever know."

That makes me feel better. "Promise?"

"Promise," he answers, looking down into my eyes, holding my stare. "You're safe with me."

Those are words I should not listen to, but I do. "I don't want to be a princess," I say to him. "I just want to be a woman who gets to sleep with a hot guy and not have to worry that he wants my brother's company more than he wants me."

I should not have told him that. Shit.

He slides off me and I think that I've completely fucked this up as he sits up. "Trust me, luv," he says and then he climbs back on top of me, but this time, with his face over my hips, his hips settling over my face. "You are far more rare, more beautiful, than a real estate company."

And then he licks down over my clit again.

It feels even better from this angle, and my whole body goes rigid, my legs jerking as I slide my mouth around his cock.

The way he's working my clit, I sink down his shaft with no warmup, swallowing him down further than I ever thought possible.

"Jesus Christ, Bella," he rumbles right against my clit and even that has my legs shaking.

I think I might forget to breathe as stars form behind my eyes, but it's so good.

I slide back up him, drawing a deep breath as I swallow him down again. I actually feel a vibration down his shaft, and I know that means he's getting close too.

I don't know much about sex, but I do understand that Gris's reaction to me is as strong as mine is to him.

That thought triggers my orgasm. I can't even really moan, his cock filling my mouth, but I give it a good try as I break apart, my lips and tongue losing any art as I just try to breathe.

It's messy and so amazing as Gris pumps in and out of my mouth several more times before he cums too, the thick liquid shooting down my throat.

I swallow it all. I know it's not normal, but I just like it, and when he's done, I collapse back on the bed, an absolute puddle, my bones melted.

Do men not have that same reaction? He spins around, drawing me close as he settles in the bed, wrapping me in a cocoon of his body.

"Do you have to..." I start to say and then feel the emotion I've been pushing down all day, rise to the surface. "Will you leave again this time?"

"I'm not going anywhere," he rumbles back.

I'd like to think it's because he cares, but I have to be prepared for the fact that it might just be because he's got some other plan.

I don't care tonight.

Even if I'm careening toward heartbreak, and I likely am, my world has been so cold.

And Gris, he is red-hot.

I snuggle deeper into him, warm and safe for the first time in what feels like forever. "I want it to be you," I whisper into the night.

"Me?"

"My first time. I want it to be you."

"Oh, it's going to be me, luv. Don't doubt that. It's going to be me."

I drift off to sleep.

When I wake the next morning, I'm still warm and snug, not having moved all night. I have no idea what time it is, but the sun is high in the sky.

I stretch my legs and bump into the rougher skin of Gris's leg, his hair ticking my smooth calf.

A smile curves my lips. He stayed.

"Morning, Bella," he rumbles behind me.

"Morning," I answer, my smile only growing. "What time is it?"

"Nine," he murmurs back before he kisses my neck. "How'd you sleep?"

"So good," I don't want to move, I'm so comfortable. "You?"

"Excellent. I like your bed."

I laugh. "It's all right. It's definitely better when there's two people in it."

He chuckles in my ear. "If that's an invitation to sleep here again, I accept."

I laugh back. I should say no, but I don't want to. How can Gris be the cause of so many of my problems and my one comfort in all of this.

I stretch again, my behind pushing into the cradle of his hips, his stiff cock settling in the crack.

"Fuck, Bella." His hand splays out on my stomach, pushing me even tighter against him. "You'd better be careful or—"

A loud knock sounds on my door. I lift my head, my brows scrunching together. This is becoming a habit…

I close my eyes and ignore the sound. Maybe whoever it is will just go away.

"Bella," Preston bellows. "I know you're in there. Open the door."

"Crap," I mutter, not moving. I don't want to get up and I definitely don't want to answer the door.

"This is usually the moment where you jump up, demand that I hide, and frantically cover the evidence."

His words sting something deep inside. But it has nothing to do with Preston being at the door. I'm over any guilt I might have felt. "You've done this before?"

I'm asking if he's had an affair with a "taken" woman.

He skates his hand from my belly over my hip, kissing my neck. "Demand that you end your engagement and then place myself in your bed? Nope. First time."

When he says it like that, it sounds like a crime of passion and not corporate blackmail. But the words still push me out of the bed as I toss the covers over him. "Feel free to stay put."

"Bella!" Preston bangs again.

"Coming!" I know Gris has seen me naked, but I still heat as I walk over to my closet naked. I feel his gaze follow me.

Not bothering with underwear, I pull on sweatpants and a hoodie. I haven't brushed my teeth or my hair, but I don't think Preston is waiting much longer.

Padding across the room, Gris is up on one elbow, his gaze assessing. "So I don't need to hide in the closet?"

"Nope. Virgin, remember? Preston has not seen the inside of my bedroom and he won't today."

"What a fucking d-bag."

That makes me smile. The word d-bag sounds so strange in his accent, and my lips are still turned up as I leave the bedroom and close the door behind me. Padding in my bare feet, I unlock the door and open it.

Preston looks absolutely livid. "What the fuck?"

"Good morning to you too," I huff back.

"You are supposed to be at the airfield, flying to Colorado with my mother."

Shit. I completely forgot. And also... I drop my voice to just above a whisper. "I'm supposed to go plan a wedding we just called off?"

"Don't be stupid. I didn't mean it."

I stare at him, shaking my head. "I meant it, Preston."

He absolutely glares at me as he takes out his phone, pushing a few buttons before he brings it to his ear. "Mum, go without Bella. She's not feeling well. High fever."

My mouth drops open. "You're not being serious?"

"We need to have a talk," Preston pushes his way past me and inside the apartment.

"We already talked."

"I was just annoyed with you. I didn't mean the words."

"You don't even like me," I reply, and the truth of those words settle over me. Why haven't I said them, thought them, much sooner? "Whatever initial spark there was between us died before we even got engaged."

Preston stares at me, his eyes widening. Did he not expect me to argue? Whatever he's thinking, he steps up to me, wrapping his hands around my upper arms. I try to jerk away but his grip is tight as he pulls me close, his hands painfully squeezing my arms as he spits in my ear. "I'm going to pretend you didn't say that. I've told the whole world we're getting married, and you will not embarrass me now."

He gives me another hard squeeze, a cry falls from my lips, and then he finally lets me go and strides toward the door without another word. Just before he leaves, he turns to me. "Don't make me get Mason involved in this."

"My brother is your big threat?" I cross my arms, hugging myself. I don't know when Preston decided he trumped me in my own family, but if that's where he wants to take the fight, I think I'm ready.

He slams the door as he goes.

CHAPTER THIRTEEN

Gris

I push out of the bed, sliding on my boxer briefs and walk toward the door. I can hear the low thrum of voices but not the words.

Bella is speaking softly, but Preston's voice grates down my spine as I hear him say, "Don't make me get Mason involved in this."

I know Mason, so I know that he loves the women in his life. He treats his wife like a goddess, and he's gone to great lengths to keep his sister out of this life until now.

Which is why I suspect he's so eager to have Preston join the family. Luke isn't seeing it, but I think Mason wants Preston to run Bella's shares as an insulator.

It's even occurred to me a few times that Mason is going to use Preston's contacts and then dispose of the man in some way, shape, or form. Maybe he's a scapegoat…

Because that's the other thing I understand about Mason. He's a man who gets the job done by any means necessary.

And then Bella's front the door slams. Loudly.

I'm out of the bedroom and down the hall in a flash.

Bella's back is to me, her arms wrapped around herself. One hand lifts and she swipes at her eyes.

"Bella?"

She doesn't turn. "Leave me alone, Gris."

Fuck. "What happened?"

"Nothing," she whispers before she turns and brushes past me, heading for her room.

I follow, determined to find out what that fucking prick did to upset her so much. Not so I can use it to my advantage. Maybe that should be what I'm thinking.

Instead, I just want to know how hard I'm punching that asswipe in the face.

"Go home, Gris," she says as she reaches the bathroom. "I know what I said this morning about..." She waves her hand, and I catch her profile, the tears shining in her eyes. "But I don't think we should see each other anymore."

"Do you feel guilty because you're cheating?"

That makes her pause. She shakes her head back and forth. "I'm not cheating."

Air rushes from my lungs. Did she just break it off with him? Is that why he slammed the door?

"Then why can't we see each other?"

"Because..." I see her face spasm in pain. "You're using me, just the same as him."

And then she slips into the bathroom, closing the door behind her.

Her words make my chest ache.

The worst part. They're true. Or at least they were. I hear the shower start and I lift my hand, knocking on the door. "Let me in, Bella."

"No."

"I have a few things I need to say to you."

"I don't want to talk."

I don't know what Preston did or said to upset her so quickly, but I'm going to find out. "I heard Preston say he was going to tattle to your brother. Even I know Mason well enough to know that he would never take Preston's side over yours. Not unless he's working some plan."

The shower turns off.

And then the knob twists.

"What kind of plan?"

She's holding the sweatshirt in front of her chest, the door only open enough that I can see about four inches of her face. "Look. I know Mason can be a real hard ass. No one knows that better than me. But he loves you and Charlotte. Of that, I am absolutely certain. And I don't think he'd let you marry a man if that man would make you miserable. Not even for Kincaid Enterprises."

"Please," she says, her voice dripping with disdain. "You know as well as I do that he needs Preston's contacts."

I did know that. The door opens a little wider and I catch a glimpse of Bella's upper arm. Which is all red and angry.

Anger pulses through me.

Pushing the door open, Bella stumbles back.

Sure enough, her other arm is also red with clear finger marks appearing. "He put his hands on you?" I practically spit the words and Bella's eyes widen in fear.

"Gris?"

I'm scaring her. Drawing in three or four deep breaths, I take a slow step toward her. "It's all right, luv. I'd never hurt you. But I want you to tell me what he did to leave those marks on your arms."

She shakes her head and that's when the tears start to fall. "He was angry and he grabbed me."

I wrap my arms around her, pulling her into my chest. That fucker is going to pay. And I mean hard.

I feel it deep in my bones. No one touches her. No one hurts her. My teeth are grinding together

Not even Mason.

Whatever plan he's got for her, I was already going to fuck it up. But now... I'm fucking it up because I'm going to protect Bella.

I don't know what it means for my family or hers, but everything else fades away. They don't matter. Not like she does.

I know I'm losing my grip. If my family doesn't kill me, hers definitely will. But I'm not sure I care. What matters is keeping her from harm.

"Sweetheart," I whisper close to her ear. "If he shows up here again, you don't let him in. You hear me?"

"Yes."

"You call me. Or you call Luke. You wait for one of us to come protect you."

"You… you'd do that? But…" I know what she's thinking. That me confronting Preston would mean she was outed. It would serve my agenda.

"Call Luke, Leo, or Roman if you're worried about your brothers finding out about me. But just don't let him in your apartment."

She nods against my chest, and I reach between us, grabbing the sweatshirt and tossing it to the floor.

Then I hook the waistband of her sweatpants and pull them down over her hips. Lifting her, I carry her into the walk-in shower, turning on the hot water before I shuck off my own briefs.

Grabbing the soap, I start washing her, my hands gently gliding over her skin. I'd like to stay here all day, but it's time I made some new plans.

Because the one I had… it isn't working.

I went and I climbed in bed with the enemy. And I plan on staying there for a while yet, anyway.

Bella is quiet, her body soft as I turn her and wash her from head to toe. With her back to me, I pull her against my chest and kiss her neck. "I promise you that I will protect you. I'm not letting anyone hurt you."

She shakes her head. "Mason tied me to Preston. Luke hitched me to you. I'm in the middle of the war and I think I'm going to be ripped apart."

My eyes close. "No."

Despite the hot water, I feel her shiver. I hold her close, promises dancing on my tongue. I don't say them.

Not yet.

I need to think this through, and I need to plan.

Or maybe I don't. Maybe the answer has always been very simple.

It's time I talked to my brothers.

I don't rush out of the shower or Bella's apartment, though. I spend the next hour keeping Bella in my arms. I need her to trust me.

I'm not sure what's coming next, because she's right. We're in the middle of a war. But I know I've got the strength and cunning to see her through.

If she'll let me…

CHAPTER FOURTEEN

ARABELLA

WHEN GRIS FINALLY LEAVES, I call Luke back.

Because we've got a few things that need to be said.

I have no idea if Gris was being so careful with me because he actually cares or because he wants exactly what Preston wants, a piece of Kincaid Enterprises.

I'm young, I'm inexperienced. But if I was naïve, I'm not anymore. Still, I think it best if I don't divulge too many details to Luke about what Gris and I have been doing.

Gris and I have a mutual destruction arrangement, which I appreciate. I'm not tipping my hand yet.

Look at me getting all savvy.

I pick up the phone and call Luke. He picks up on the first ring. "Bug."

"I think it might be time to retire my childhood nickname." I'm in sweats still. Preston told his mother I was sick, so I find myself with a free day. I think I'll use it. "We both know I'm not your Bug anymore."

"Bella," Luke whispers, sounding pained. "I just wanted to protect you."

"Is that what you're telling yourself?" I scoff. "You sent the man who wants revenge on Mason right to my door."

He's silent.

"What did you think might happen?"

"He's got a certain way with the ladies. I thought he might show you there were other options besides Preston."

I shake my head. "You sent a playboy..." I ought to remember that, because that's exactly what Gris is. "To break up my impending marriage. Ask yourself, and I want you to really listen to the answer... how are you better than Mason?" And then I hang up.

Luke doesn't call back.

But now I'm pacing around my apartment, and I finally change out of my sweats and put on a little pair of shorts and a tank top. The marks on my arms have faded.

I pull my hair into a ponytail and grab my purse, running to the grocery store and grabbing some of my favorite foods. Stuff I haven't been eating, because of the wedding.

Then, when I'm back, I eat a nice lunch, a giant chocolate chip cookie, and change into my bathing suit, heading out to the apartment pool.

I've got pale skin, unlike my brothers, so I bring sunblock, I'm not looking to burn myself. I just need some quiet time.

That's when my phone rings.

No one is out here, I'm alone, but I still groan when I see Mason's name pop up on my screen.

Mason is a force. Unlike Luke, who took my anger, I'm not sure how this is going to go.

But today's the day for it, so I pick up. "Hey, Mason."

"Arabella," his deep voice reverberates through the phone. "You left early last night."

"I..." I take a deep breath. "I'm not marrying Preston."

Silence meets my words.

"I'll keep up the pretense if you want me to, at least for another week, but no more." There. I've said the words.

"What's changed?"

"What?" I expected him to refuse. Or yell.

"What has changed? I know it's something. You've been different since you got back…"

I look down at the phone. I know I hit Luke with that comment about him being like Mason, but Luke would never talk to me like this. He would appeal to my heart, not try to get inside my head. In the past, I've crumbled during conversations like this with Mason. But I don't want to. Not this time. "I'll answer your question if you answer mine. What happened between you and Luke?"

"I told you—" he grits between his teeth.

"You haven't told me anything. And I don't know why I should share with you when won't with me."

"Christ, Arabella." Frustration colors every syllable.

But he isn't the only one who has had enough. "I'm not marrying him for Kincaid. I'm not going to be fodder for the company."

"Is that what you think I would do?"

"It's what you did to Luke, isn't it?" The words fly out before I can stop them.

Mason lets out a string of curses. "Did Luke tell you that?"

"Of course not. Luke would never do that."

Mason is silent again. I know he's doing mental math.

"I'll attend a few more events in the coming week if you need me to, but work quickly to gain those investors you need."

"You do not get to tell me how to run the business."

"And you don't get to tell me who I should marry."

He curses again. "We can't afford Luke's shares. I've invested all of our capital and more into the tunnel."

I never hear Mason talk like this. I know I have been a beneficiary of Kincaid Enterprises. I've given nothing back. It's why I've been silent for so long as this whole situation has unfolded with Preston. "I'll help however I can, Mason. But I can't marry Preston. We don't even like each other and I think he might actually hate me."

"Why would you say that?"

"I don't know. He can't even fake being nice to me. All he does is yell and sneer all the time. I'm not even sure why he asked me to marry him, though if I were to guess, it was probably to gain access to the company."

Mason rumbles into the phone.

"And I only said yes because I was afraid. But I need to stop making decisions based on what scares me."

"Bella," Mason draws in a deep breath. "If I'd known any of this..."

"I get it, Mason. I don't mean to make your life more difficult."

"Let me consider our options. Just don't do anything."

Everybody is thinking. Making plans. While I'm supposed to sit here and wait. I click off my phone, setting it back in my bag.

I think I'm tired of waiting. It's time for me to make some plans of my own.

CHAPTER FIFTEEN

GRIS

DRIVING from Arabella's I call my brother Tris. "Are you home?"

"No. I'm at the office."

"All right. I'll meet you there in fifteen." I need this conversation to be reasonably private, but that can be achieved in Tris's office or my own.

Tris manages far more of the daily operations of the company.

Killian is our muscle.

I am the face. And by that I mean, I shake the hands, I negotiate at bars, and on the golf course.

I use a combination of charm, intelligence, a will made of iron to seal any deal I set my mind to closing. My lack of emotional involvement, however, makes it all possible.

It's part of why what happened with Mason Kincaid pisses me off so much. I never lose like that.

Then again, losing has brought Arabella into my arms.

I give my head a little shake. What has gotten into me?

My phone rings, Luke's name flashing on the screen. "What's up?"

"What the fuck is going on between you and my sister?"

"What did she say?" I flex my fingers on the wheel. Even asking that question is a tell that there are secrets.

"She said to talk to you."

So. She's keeping our deal of mutual destruction. She didn't rat me out. "There's nothing to say."

"She also said I'm no better than Mason by sending a playboy to manipulate her."

Those words hurt more than they should. Granted, that was completely my intent, and I made her break it off with Preston.

"Listen. I am not manipulating your sister. I am about to speak with my family because…" I rarely misstep when it comes to a negotiation. But I cannot decide if I should tell Luke I'm considering marrying Arabella myself.

I can't see the path. Will he be relieved or livid? I never misstep like this and, as if I need more evidence, I am getting emotionally entangled and it's clouding my judgment.

But maybe that's because I shouldn't talk to Luke at all. Arabella is the person I should speak with first.

"Because?"

I sigh. "Because Arabella broke it off with Preston."

"I know. She told me. Right after she accused me of being no better than Mason." I can hear the hurt in his voice. Luke is chill. Nothing bothers him. But Arabella's anger clearly has him riled.

She's like that, I guess. Able to get under the thickest skin. "She is pissed at you."

"You weren't supposed to tell her we were friends."

"I…" I swallow down a lump. "I quickly realized that lies were not going to get us where we needed to go."

Luke lets out a long breath. "At least she broke up with that complete piece of shit. She doesn't need to get married if she doesn't want. Mason is not pushing her into that. If it's the last thing I ever do for her, I'll give her that freedom."

I frown. There are a million reasons for me to tense at his words. But one of the biggest… it puts me and Luke on a crash course of interests. Not to mention, if Arabella doesn't take over the shares, Mason just has more power. "Look, Luke…" I don't want to lie to him. I think I'm tired of playing the sides against each other.

Which might be the craziest thing I've ever thought. I love this game.

"Yeah?"

"Arabella is drowning. She's not meant to be in the middle of all this. It's not her nature."

I've known some women who are titans of the industry. I admire the fuck out of them. But that's just not my girl. And it doesn't matter to me, I'm a guy with enough drive for both of us. I like how she's soft enough to temper all my hard edges.

"I know it," he says, in a tired voice. "I swear that Mason is doing all of this to force me back in the company."

The light bulb goes off. That's exactly what Mason is doing. From involving Arabella to backing Preston, Mason wants Luke back in the fold and Arabella is Luke's weak point. I smile as I pull into a spot.

Because a new plan is beginning to form. "What if that is what he wants?"

"I won't fucking do it."

Tris is going to kill me. "What if you sold your shares to me?"

Luke pauses. I know what he's thinking. Much as he likes me, Mason does not. If Luke sells to me, in Mason's eyes, Luke will have let the enemy right into the heart of Kincaid. There would be no going back.

"I've got to think on that one."

We hang up as I pull into our office building. It's not nearly as big or impressive as Kincaid Enterprise's high-rise in the heart of Vegas, but then again, I save our money for what really matters.

I stride to the elevators, making my way to our fourth-floor office. Smiling at the receptionist, I pass by several employees, making my way to Tris's office. His assistant stands. "Mr. Smith."

I know Jeff will probably try and stop me. Tris doesn't like unexpected visitors. "He knows I'm coming." I wink at the man and keep walking, because I don't like to be delayed and I don't really care what my brother likes or doesn't like. The beauty of family.

Tris is sitting at his desk, on his phone. "No, Killian, I don't think there is time for you to do a big game hunt in Africa this month."

"Tell that fucker to keep his shit together," I rumble. Killian is incredibly good at his job and loyal to the core.

But even as his brother, I know that guy's not quite right. He likes killing things way too much.

Tris switches his phone to speaker.

"Yeah, Gris is here, and as usual, he's a merry ray of fucking sunshine."

I quirk a half smile. "Hearts and fucking roses. That's me."

Tris laughs and so does Killian. "Keep my shit together, huh?" Killian grouses. "Don't say I didn't warn you if I don't."

"Are you about to go off the deep end?"

"Maybe."

Fuck. We don't need another variable in play here. I look at Tris, who's got his teeth gritted. "Gris, how are things with the Kincaids?"

I run a hand through my hair. "You know how in every plan shit seems to fall apart before it comes together?"

"Fuck," Tris rumbles.

"I'm working on several plays," I hold up my hands. "Not sure which one I'm leaning into yet."

Tris mutes the phone. "Send him away or keep him here?"

If things get ugly, I might need him. I reach over and unmute the phone on the desk. "Kill, can you hang in Vegas another week? There might be some dirty work here."

I practically hear Killian's blood rising. "Yeah. I can hang."

"So, tell us about all the options," Tris will not be swayed by Killian's bloodlust. He wants information from me, but I'm not sure how much I want to give.

"Arabella has broken it off with Preston, leaving Mason vulnerable." I force myself to sound casual.

Tris's mouth falls open.

"I'm considering buying Luke's shares."

"No fucking way," Tris rumbles. He knows it would wipe us out of cash. To be clear, we would not go in debt the way Mason has. But we would be cash poor, which will limit future options. "And why would he sell to you?"

I haven't told my brothers that Luke and I are friends. And that Luke is how I got access to Arabella in Hawaii. "Because he's as pissed at Mason as we are." I hadn't told them that either.

"You've got a lot of information on this one," Tris cocks his head.

"That's my job," I answer evenly.

"You know a lot, even for you." Tris suspects the truth. I've got an insider. Actually, I've got two.

I push to standing again. "Either way, the engagement is dissolving as planned, which means Mason is about to make a move. We need to be ready."

Tris stands but his gaze is skeptical. "You said you had multiple plans."

We stare at each for several beats before I finally pull my shoulders straighter. "I'm considering marrying Arabella myself."

Both my brothers explode at the same moment. I can't hear what Killian says over the phone because Tris is loudly spitting a wild string of curses.

"If Preston Wingate can do it, why can't I?"

But Tris shakes his head, giving me a skeptical glare. "You were acting weirdly possessive at the benefit. You haven't… developed feelings, have you?"

"I don't have feelings," I reply. "I'm like Killian, only sane."

"I resent that," Killian grumps back. "I have loads of feelings. It's controlling them that I struggle with."

Both Tris and I look down at his phone, as Tris scoffs. "I suppose anger counts as an emotion."

"Fuck you both," Killian says and hangs up.

"You pissed him off." I'm trying to change the subject.

"Everything pisses him off," Tris answers. "I'd rather talk about you. I don't think this marriage plan is a good idea."

"It's an excellent idea. It's why Wingate proposed."

"Yeah, but..." He leans forward. "You're too invested."

"How the fuck would you know?"

He drops his chin, his gaze narrowing as his lip curls. "Let me marry her instead."

"Fuck that." The words are out before I can stop them. It's a mistake. I should have played it like I didn't care, but I can't. The very idea of my brother touching Arabella has me crawling out of my skin.

Tris shows his teeth. "You are catching feelings. How the fuck is that possible?"

I could deny it. But instead, I stand, "I've got a handle on this. We'll get what we need. You know you can always count on me."

Tris starts to argue but I'm done talking. Did I say the noose was tightening around Arabella's neck? I'm no better.

Plans and allegiances are shifting on every side. But that's all right.

I was made for this. I don't know how I'm winning yet, but I will. Because it's never been more important that I don't lose. It's not just my life at stake, but Arabella's too.

CHAPTER SIXTEEN

Arabella

The sun is hot and even after dipping into the pool, I'm starting to sweat. I'm just about to go inside when my phone rings.

My eyes widen in surprise. It's Gris. "Hey."

"Hey, gorgeous, where are you?"

"Where are you?" I smile nipping at my lip. After talking with Mason, it's just nice to hear his voice.

"Outside your apartment door, but you're not answering."

I give a half sigh even as my smile grows. "Mrs. Gillette is going to have a fit."

"Who's that?"

"My next-door neighbor. People have started banging on my door several times a day." I lean back in the chair. "She's going to file a complaint for sure."

"Now that is a problem I can take care of for you," he rumbles into the phone. "And you still haven't told me where you are."

"Why do you want to know?" I know I'm being difficult. But it's fun. I might like the way Gris chases me.

"Because I want to kiss you."

"Good answer. I'm down by the pool."

He hangs up without a word and I stare at my phone. That little game of cat and mouse ended quickly. But a minute later, Gris is striding across the pool deck.

I'm in a small white bikini, covered in sunblock, and sweaty from the sun. My hair is in a high ponytail and my feet are bare. I look nothing like the polished woman in heels and a silk gown, and I'm intimately aware that he is draped in an expensive Armani suit.

He looks every inch the powerful aristocrat as he strides toward me. I touch my messy ponytail, nipping at my lip. "I wasn't expecting guests."

He keeps moving toward me. "I noticed."

Does he not like it? "I can..."

"You look hot as fuck, Bella. I'm just glad there aren't any other men out here, I'd have to kill them."

My teeth slip off my lip as I smile. "Oh." Does he know what he does to me when he says stuff like that? Appreciates me like that? "Is that why you're here? To kill random men?"

He chuckles. "No. I only came to run my hands over your skin. And the fact that you're in a bathing suit makes that very easy."

"Gris," I lightly groan. He's going to wreck me, talking like that. "This is so complicated..."

And I promised my brother I'd pretend at being engaged for a few more days at least. I can't keep letting Gris in my bed. Can I?

Because while I didn't feel that guilty about Preston, I kind of hate that I'm going behind my brother's back. Or should I say brothers' backs. I don't think Luke would be very happy either if he knew what Gris and I have been doing.

"It's not complicated, princess. Not for you."

"Not for me?"

"You let me touch you all over. I get to listen to your sweet little moans and your begging cries and then..." His lips press into a firm line. "You let me be your soldier."

I frown. That requires a certain level of trust we don't have. I trust him with my body, I know that. But my life, I'm not so sure.

And the lives of my brothers, particularly Mason. I know for a fact that Gris is the last man I can trust. "You can't be my soldier if the person you most want to fight is Mason." I turn away to look at the pool.

He's silent, but he sits on the edge of my chair, his hand running up my leg until it reaches the edge of my bikini bottom. He's so close to my… I feel my body tense up, my muscles flexing in a way that makes me ache between my legs.

And then he slides his hand over my mound, the tips of his fingers just grazing my clit. "Are you trying to say I have to choose my family or yours?"

I shake my head, my hair brushing my shoulders. "I'd never ask you to do that. They're your family."

He leans in then, kissing that spot behind my ear that makes me shiver. "You wouldn't?"

"They're your partners, Gris. Your brothers. Family should stay together. Luke should…" I stop. I'm saying too much.

He rumbles in a way I don't understand. Does he agree, not agree? He stands back up, and for a second, I think he's going to leave, that I've pushed him away.

Which was my intent.

But it still stings. He reaches a hand down, and after only a moment's hesitation, I slip my fingers into his. He helps me from my chair and reaches into my bag, pulling out my cover-up.

I cock my head to the side in question.

"Put it on," he growls out in response.

"But I'm not done tanning."

"First, you don't need to tan. Your skin is gorgeous. And secondly, soldier or no, I'm taking you upstairs and bending you over the bed until you scream my name. Licking your pussy is my new favorite pastime and I've gone too long already."

I'm absolutely drenched in a second as he yanks the little strapless dress over my head, settling it over my bathing suit.

I barely have time to grab my flip flops and bag before he's yanking me toward the doors.

"Gris," I give a breathless giggle. "At least let me get my shoes on."

His response is to put an arm around my shoulder blades and then, in an arching stoop, hook another under my knees, pulling me into his arms so that he's carrying me. "Good lord, man, I can walk."

"I like carrying you," he says, like that's an explanation, and pushes the door open while still holding onto me.

The moment the elevator door closes, his lips find mine, his tongue sliding between my lips as he devours my mouth.

This is my apartment building. Any resident could step into this elevator with us, but I'm not sure I care as he tips my head back a little further, our tongues tangling.

The elevator dings and I yank my mouth away, gasping for breath.

I must look like I've been ravaged, but no one enters. We're on my floor.

Striding down the hall, he only sets me down so I can fish out my keys from my bag.

That's when Mrs. Gillette yanks open the door. Gris is turned toward me, mostly blocking her from my view, but I catch her gaze over his shoulder. "How many times is someone going to bang on your door, young lady?"

But she stops the moment her eyes land on Gris's back. His very broad back.

Subtly, he shifts his cock and then, slides a hand in his pocket, before he turns to face her. "You must be Mrs. Gillette."

"Oh," she says, sounding like a smitten schoolgirl the way her voice gets all breathless and her eyes turn glassy. "Why, yes."

"I'm so sorry for the noise." Gris must flash her a smile the way she grins back. "That Preston is proving to be a real thorn." Then he pulls out a business card. "This is my personal number. If he shows up here making noise, you call me. Any time. Day or night and I will come take care of him."

"Oh," Mrs. Gillette says again, and this time, she clutches her pearls. She. Clutches. Her. Pearls. "I will."

I unlock the door and step inside, Gris giving Mrs. Gillette a warm goodbye before he follows.

"That is why I can't trust you. You're too Hugh Grant."

"Hugh Grant is not titled," he grouses back. "And I did that for you. If Preston shows his face around here, I want to know."

I drop my bag and my flip flops and then pull down the cover up, letting it fall on the kitchen floor.

Then I pull out the elastic holding my hair as I start for the bedroom. I let my hair fall down as walk and then I give it a little fluff. "You're a giver, Gris Smith."

"Damn right I am."

My back to him, I untie my bikini top and let it drop too. "Come give some more to me."

He makes this noise that reverberates through his chest, and it makes me ache, it's so masculine. And then I hear his footsteps tap across the floor as he follows.

I pick up the pace, wrapping an arm around my bare breasts, as I break out into a run, giving a giggle as I reach my room. He moves faster too, but I almost make it to the bed before he catches me, his arms coming around me as he lifts me off the ground. "That was fucking hot."

It was. I'm dripping down my thighs, my body humming. "Next time, we'll play hide and seek."

He grabs the string on the side of my hip and tugs, the string coming undone, the bottoms half falling off. Then he plunges his fingers between my legs.

I cry out, it feels so good, my toes curling as the muscles of my thighs flex. "Gris," I gasp out. "Oh God."

He takes the last step to the bed and then sets me down on my belly, my legs hanging over the side.

"Don't move," he commands as he yanks at his own clothing. I catch the pale blue of his dress shirt as it hits the floor.

And then his mouth covers my seam, as he licks me from one end to the other. "Oh God," I cry out, the friction so good as I fist the blankets. "Yes."

He licks me, even as he uses one hand to undo his belt buckle, I hear the clank before the sound of zipper fills the room.

Is he planning on pushing inside me from behind? I'm pretty sure I wouldn't object. I want to feel Gris inside me.

But he doesn't.

He eases back and then I feel nothing. Lifting up, I look over my shoulder…

CHAPTER SEVENTEEN

Gris

Every time we're together, Bella sheds more of her inhibitions, the sex getting hotter and hotter.

She's bent over, completely exposed to me.

Her hair is streaming over one shoulder, her lips puffy and her eyes glazed over as she looks over her shoulder at me. "Please, Gris. Don't stop. You feel so good."

My cock swells in my hand. Yeah. I'm jacking it like a teenager. I know I can't take her virginity like this.

And I know I'm fucking losing it, because part of me wants to make her promise to be my wife before I break her open.

I reach my hand between her legs rubbing her with one hand, myself with another as I just stare.

Sex in the full light of day allows me to map every freckle, ever indent, and I want to know her intimately. I want to know her as well as I know myself.

It's like she's an extension of me.

Which is so crazy because we've only known each other for a few days.

She rolls her hips, purring like a cat.

I let go of my cock, spreading her wide before I slide my thumb down the crack of her ass, circling her little brown hole.

I feel the jolt of desire that courses through her. Does she like that? Good. "This. You. They're mine. You're mine. No one else touches you, do you hear me?"

She pushes against my hand. "No one but you."

"Good girl." I lean over her, nipping at the spot where her shoulder meets her neck. "Now tell me how you want to cum, baby."

"I want it however you give it," she purrs back.

Fuck. Me. I reach under her, sliding my hand between the bed and her belly until I make it to her clit, then I press.

She bucks, crying out.

Then, because I'm a masochist, I let the tip of my cock slide between her folds. I sink into her, not going far.

I'm playing at fucking her.

But even the tip being inside her feels amazing. She clenches around me, trying to pull me in deeper which pulls a low groan from my chest.

I grab my cock with my other hand, pumping it again. It's as close as I can come to fucking her without really sinking inside her.

Next time.

Next time, I'll tease her until she promises to be just mine, mine forever, and then I'll sink so deep inside her, I'll brand her as mine alone.

But right now… I can't tease because we're both careening toward the end, her body shaking under mine.

"That's it," I force the words out between gritted teeth. This is why I can't stay away. It's too good. "Fuck, Bella, baby, cum for me, sweetheart. Cum all over me."

She breaks apart on a broken sob, her body following my command without question.

My own cum erupts from my cock, and I just manage to pull out, spraying hot cum all over her ass crack.

It's dirty and hot and I'm still pumping cum into the crevice when I slide my thumb through the mess, spreading it evenly over her skin.

I'm marking my fucking territory.

"Baby," I say, my voice unusually rough with emotion. I'm bending over her back. "I appreciate what you said about my family. And I know how you feel about yours. But neither changes what I'm going to do for you. For us."

"What are you going to do for us?"

I finally let my cock go, my hand sliding up the silky skin of her back. "I'm going to protect you.... Keep you safe."

She draws in a deep breath as she lays her cheek over her folded arms. "I'm trying to be strong, Gris. But I don't even know who to trust."

I hear the tremor, and it breaks me. I nuzzle her ear, pressing my chest to her back. "You can trust me. I promise."

I feel the rigidity returning to her muscles. "Except we both know I can't, Gris. We started this with you telling me that you'd tell my whole family about Hawaii if I didn't end my engagement."

That is true. "Things have changed."

She shakes her head, her hair tickling my nose. "I don't want to stop. You make me feel so good. And I trust you with my body. Implicitly. But with everything else..."

My eyes slide closed. "If you can trust me with your body, maybe it's telling you that you can trust me, period."

"I don't..."

"Think about it. Have you ever put any faith in Preston?"

She's silent and I know I made a point she's considering. But I also understand that it might be time I didn't just tell.

It might be time I showed her that she can trust me.

It's going to require a rather large gesture. I don't know quite what it will be yet, but I do know that whatever it is, my family is likely going to kill me.

Then again, I'm a smart guy. I make plans happen. Am I big enough and tough enough, smart enough, to thread the needle between the Kincaids and the Smiths?

We're all about to find out.

CHAPTER EIGHTEEN

ARABELLA

I PULL my car out of the garage, the setting Vegas sun shining into my eyes as I pull on my sunglasses. Traffic is heavy, and I ought to pay attention, but my thoughts are filled with how I spent my afternoon.

I heard what Gris said about trusting him.

I've got to be honest. I want to believe him. But also... I really understand I shouldn't. Mason is my brother, and I love him, and he loves me too. Even knowing that, I also understand that his plans can and have backfired on all of us.

But Gris, he's built exactly like Mason. He is a planner, a manipulator. Only he isn't my brother. If Mason sometimes forgets to factor in my feelings, if his ambitions get in the way, what might Gris do? Even if he really cares, I might end up crushed by Gris's schemes and strength.

And if he doesn't care about me...

Well, then I am for sure in for a world of hurt. I can't even resist an afternoon tryst with him. I can't deny him anything.

I shiver again, sliding the air conditioning vent to point away from me. I said I was going to do some scheming of my own, and I have.

I invited both Mason and Luke out to dinner tonight.

They have no idea that they're both attending. I would like to pursue things with Gris, but first I need to right things with my family. It's the only way I can move forward, knowing that what I've got going on with Gris isn't going to come back on them.

Mason picked the restaurant, which happens to be inside our luxury hotel, Chateau Blanc. The restaurant, which features French cuisine is called Cheval Blanc, and it's normally my favorite place to eat. I've been avoiding it because Preston currently stays on this property. Mason offered him an apartment, but I think he's enjoying the perks of being in a hotel attached to our family.

I pull up the car and hand the keys to the valet. Tonight, I'm in a strapless pale pink dress that falls just below my knees and strappy sandals.

The bit of sun I got today has kissed my skin and I curled my hair the way a warrior might add war paint.

Okay, maybe it's a bit different.

But I wanted to look as feminine as possible. Remind my brothers that I am their beloved sister, not the rope in a game of tug of war.

I enter the lobby of the hotel to find that both Mason and Luke have already arrived.

They stand facing each other, matching glares, each with their arms crossed. I sigh. But also… it's good to see them together.

"Hello," I call out with a wave.

They both swing their gazes to me. It's hard to know which one looks more pissed. "You set a trap?" Mason rumbles.

"Since when are family dinners traps?" I ask back as I approach and kiss Mason's cheek. Then I kiss Luke's.

"You know damn well Mason and I aren't talking," Luke says by way of greeting.

"That's all right. I've got a lot to say. You can both sit quietly and listen. But I am famished, and I love Cheval Blanc, so let's get a table. Shall we?"

Begrudgingly, they both follow. The hostess takes one look at us and with hissed words at the waiter next to her, shows us to a private room.

"We have a fourth joining us," Mason says to the hostess. "Show Preston Wingate in when he arrives."

My hackles rise, but I don't need to say a word, Luke is spitting them all for me. "Why the fuck is that fucking prick joining us?"

"He would like a chance to speak with Bella," Mason replies, taking a seat.

I huff out a breath. "You're a dirty rat, you know that, Mason? This is why people don't like you. I was completely clear this afternoon. I'm not marrying him, and I don't want to speak to him."

That other plan I had, where I just get on a plane, is sounding even better.

"I'm not the only one who used the play, 'invite unexpected guest,' am I?" he replies. "Why don't you tell us what we're here to discuss?" Mason asks like he's legitimately perplexed. Which can't be true. He must know... Mason is smart like that.

"After the food arrives," I say, just trying to gain back a bit of control.

Luke helps me into my chair, and I make a show of opening my menu like I'm actually considering. I know the menu backward and forward.

"So what are we discussing until then?" Luke grumps, also opening his menu.

"How are wedding plans coming with you and Kate?" I ask, setting my menu down again.

Luke gives the smallest smile. "Haven't planned much. I think we're going to have the ceremony in Colorado."

Mason nods. "Best place for a wedding. You can really think when surrounded by the scent of pine."

I hide my smile, remembering Mrs. Wingate's comment. But also, it's nice to hear them exchange even a single pleasantry.

"We're not having it at a resort," Luke retorts. "We're thinking her stepfather's cabin would be best."

Mason's lips press together. My guess is Mason knows the place. "And how is Charlotte," I ask, trying to move things along.

Mason runs a hand through his hair. A tell that he's nervous. "She's good."

My brows lift as I lean forward. "Really?"

"Did you talk with her?" Mason asks, leaning in too. "She says all the throwing up is normal, but I fucking hate it."

I blink back my surprise. Oh my God…. "Charlotte's pregnant?"

"She can barely keep food down," he whispers roughly. "How can I keep her safe when her own body is attacking her?"

Luke's menu is forgotten too. "Mason. It's totally normal."

He shakes his head, and I see deep worry in Mason's eyes like I've never seen before. "The doctor prescribed some medication but…"

I see Luke's eyes slide closed. "I can ask Kate…"

"Would you please?" Mason sounds pained. "I should have been more careful. I don't need to have kids. I'd be happy just me and her. I just want her to be safe. I…" He closes his mouth, likely realizing how much he's given away.

The waiter enters and I order a glass of Chardonnay along with a delicate seafood dish that is true French delicacy.

I look over at Luke and I can see the waiver in his eyes. "I know what happened between the two of you. Leo told me."

"Fucking Leo," they say in unison.

"He's going to be a better dad than me," Mason tosses in after. "Never thought I'd see the day when he beat me out at something that wasn't weightlifting."

One side of my mouth quirks up. "Mason, you're going to be a great dad. Hell, you're the closest thing to a father I've ever had. I don't know what I would have done without you."

"That's your bar for great. He's trying to get you to marry a total twat."

"Hey," Mason barks. "She said yes before I'd ever even met Preston."

"But you put all that pressure on her with my shares," Luke fires back.

"Because you're quitting just like that."

"Not like that, you tried to ruin Kate's career. No. Worse. You tried to make me do it."

I sigh and hold up my hands. "We need to find a solution that doesn't involve Preston."

Both glare at me. "I'm not making up with Mason just because you want me to, Bug."

I pinch my nose. "We are a family. If I'm about to have nieces and nephews, we're all having Christmas together. I've lost too many people, you've lost too many people—"

"Some things aren't meant to go back together." Luke's jaw could cut glass.

Blessedly, my wine arrives, and I take a long sip. Then I turn to Luke. "Did you think about my last question to you?"

"What was that?" Mason asks.

But I know Luke remembers by the way he grimaces. I asked him how he was better than Mason. Time to drive home the point. Sending Gris really messed with my life. Granted, I've been enjoying the mess, but it might have gone the other way. "You want to sell, that's one thing. You want to hurt Mason, you're hurting all of us." I point a finger at Luke.

"You're taking his side?" Luke's nostrils flare with irritation.

Good point. "I'm not marrying Preston. He's a complete prick." I turn to Mason. "And since you've given him all the power, and you did, you can tell him that you support my decision."

Mason's mouth opens and closes.

But I think I might be done with this dinner. I stand. "And as for you, Luke Kincaid. You want out, you can wait until Mason can clear the debt. Because you care about your family and are not a selfish man, correct? And you don't do things to screw them over. You're that much better than Mason." My brows lift and I see him cringe.

He's reading me loud and clear.

I toss my napkin on the table and then take another long swallow of my wine. I'll have to have that seafood dish another time.

"You two eat. And talk. And work something out that honors both your needs and Kincaid Enterprises, and the rest of the family too. And stop acting like a couple of spoiled babies."

"Spoiled babies," Mason rumbles.

"Bella," Luke stands too. "What the fuck has gotten into you…"

I point my finger right in his face. "Unlike you, I'm the forgiving type. Which is why I'm forgiving you."

"What's she talking about?"

I look back at Mason. "Be nice and I'll tell you."

"What the hell happened to my baby sister?" Mason's eyes wide with shock.

"I grew up." Picking up my clutch, I make my way to the door. Before I leave, I look back over my shoulder. "Be nice. Both of you. If you're not, I'm calling both your wives into the next family dinner, and they will make certain you behave."

And then I make my way out to the lobby. I'm smiling because I think I might have actually done it.

I might just be a Kincaid after all.

But as my gaze swings over to the elevators, I stop, my feet like cement. I can't believe my eyes…

CHAPTER NINETEEN

Arabella

I slowly pivot to make sure I'm seeing this correctly.

The lobby of the hotel is crowded, but I'd still recognize him anywhere.

Preston.

Only he isn't alone.

His back is to me, as he stands facing the wall, and over his shoulder I catch a peek of blonde hair.

Interesting.

Slowly, I start walking toward them, my ear cocked. The crowd is loud enough that I don't hear much until I'm standing right behind Preston.

"Fuck, baby, you're so hot," Preston groans, his hips pressing into hers. Is he humping her in the lobby?

It's not that I'm jealous. I'm not sure I would have been even if we were still engaged. My pride would have been wounded, but I'd have gotten over that.

I've been up to my own extracurricular activities and, if we're being honest, Preston and I never had a real relationship.

We had a few real dates. But that's about it. This whole thing was really more of a bad merger.

My arms cross as I try to figure out how to play this. I won't fake sad. But I want Preston to know that I know.

It's just one more weapon in my break-up arsenal.

I really am sounding more and more like a Kincaid. I clear my throat, but I don't think they hear me over the wet sounds of the kissing.

Gross.

No wonder I never went that far with Preston.

Taking my phone out of my clutch, I hit his name.

"Fuck," he rumbles, lifting his head long enough to look at my name on his screen and then he dismisses the call. "I'm late."

"Don't go," she whines. "Stay with me, baby. Take me upstairs."

"I already told you, Mason's going to be there. I don't give a fuck about her, but him..."

"You're not really going to marry her, are you?" She says in this pouty voice that sets my teeth on edge.

Preston kisses her again, long and sloppy, and now I feel the irritation rise. This is why he can't ever take my calls or call me when his parents come into town, because he's busy fucking some other woman. Meanwhile, he tells me over and over how I'm the one failing. Fuck him.

"Preston," I say. Loudly. "You haven't answered her question."

He lifts his head and slowly pivots, his eyes wide. "Bella."

I hear the gasp, but I don't look at her. I don't care about her. I don't really care about him either, but I have a score to settle. "Let me answer for you. No, we're not getting married. You can have him, sweetheart, but just in case he hasn't told you, he's got no money of his own. Everything he's been spending on you belongs to my family."

And then I pivot, walking with my head high across the lobby. Was that a low blow? Maybe. Did he deserve it? Definitely.

But I'm only halfway across when Preston catches up to me, his grip biting into my elbow. "Wait."

"No, thank you," I try to pull my arm from his grip, but he tightens it as he spins me. I nearly fall on my heels but just catch myself as he drops his face into mine. "We are not done."

"Yes, we are."

His grip grows painful, and it takes everything in me not to cry out. "I told you last time I dropped into your apartment that you are fucking marrying me."

"Being embarrassed that I've called off the wedding," I grit back, my teeth clenched. "That sounds like a you problem."

"It's about to be a you problem," he spits back, his saliva hitting my cheek. I close my eyes, a reflex to keep the spit out.

"Miss Kincaid," a deep voice to my right makes me snap them open again. A security guard for the hotel is only two feet away. "Do you need some assistance?"

My shoulders wilt with relief, as I look around and notice several people staring. Clearing my throat I give a small nod. "Would you be so kind as to escort me to my car?"

"Of course," he answers as Preston slowly releases me. Once I'm free, I say to the guard, "Two of my brothers are dining at Cheval Blanc, please inform them of the incident when you return."

I hear Preston spit a string of curses. I don't look back as the guard lightly takes my arm, helping me outside, my car pulling up a moment later.

When I slide in, I sigh with relief. Hitting a button on my Apple CarPlay, I order from my favorite sushi restaurant and request delivery.

I don't think I'm leaving my house again tonight.

Pulling into the garage, I sigh with relief as the elevator doors slide closed. I hope I did some good work with my brothers.

And as for Preston...

He can go to hell for all I care.

I head into my apartment, slipping off my strappy sandals, and make my way into the bedroom, to put them away.

My dinner will be here in a few minutes, so I take off the dress and pull on a pair of shorts and short T-shirt. I briefly consider just putting on pajamas, but then think better of it. I'll change again after my food is delivered.

Heading out to the kitchen, I pour myself a sparkling water and then a second glass of wine. I'm celebrating tonight, and I barely had any of my first glass.

But I've only had the first sip when a knock sounds at my door.

Setting the glass down, I pad over, glad my sushi is a little early. I'm starving.

But when I open the door, my breath stops in my lungs, because standing in front of me is *not* the delivery guy, it's Preston.

Shit.

I try to close the door, but he throws his hand up inserting his body into the opening, as he pushes the door back open again. "You didn't think you were getting away that easy, did you?"

"Preston," I start but before I can say any more, his hand comes down hard across my cheek.

Pain explodes through my face and skull as I stumble back. But he's on me in a second, his hand at my throat as he spits in my ear. "We're going to finish our conversation now, you little bitch."

I try to gasp in a breath, both my hands coming to his wrist. "Preston. Stop."

"You want to know the truth?" He spits in my face again. "I don't mind slumming it. In fact, I like a woman from the other side of the tracks, but you..." His face is twisted and angry. Ugly. "Are just a sewer rat who somehow still thinks she's better than everyone else."

"I don't think that," I push out as his other hand twists into my hair, pulling hard.

"First," he says, "you're going to let me fuck you. And then, you're going to put my ring back on and you're going to fucking smile when you tell Mason it's all been a mistake."

I try to breathe but I'm seeing stars as I tighten my grip on his wrist. I need air.

That's when his phone rings.

"Fuck," he grits out and just as suddenly as he grabbed me, he lets me go.

I crumple to the ground, gasping in deep breaths.

"Mason," Preston says by way of greeting. "I'm sorry I was late."

My brother? My brother is on the line? "Mason," I try to cry out, but my voice won't work. Not enough to be heard.

Tears fill my eyes as I curl into a ball on the floor. But that's when I feel my phone in my pocket. Tentatively, I withdraw the device, trying to hide it from Preston. I can't see, my eyes are too blurred by tears, so I push the first number in my call list. Is it Mason? Luke? I think it's Luke.

"Bella?" I hear Gris's deep baritone slide through the speaker, and I wilt in relief. I know Gris can't come here. It would ruin everything. But I need help.

"I need Luke," I whisper, my voice catching, as I cut him off.

I hear Preston talking to Mason, his back to me. "No, I'm with Bella now. Just a lover's spat. Nothing to worry about."

"I'm on my way, already. Almost there." His voice is edged with steel.

I hear Preston. "I can't put her on, Mason, she's in the bathroom. You know women and conversations like these, she's all teary."

"Is that cunt on the phone with your brother?"

"Yes," I say, but Preston must hear me because, as I'm inching by him, his hand lashes out and grabs my ankle.

I manage a hoarse cry, and I hear Mason's voice on the phone. "What the fuck was that?"

"Yapping dog in the hall," Preston answers. "Listen, I'll have Bella call you back in five. Just give us a minute to work this out."

And then he hangs up.

I keep my phone buried in my hair, even as he keeps pulling me, sliding me on my back across the floor.

Then he drops down, straddling my hips with his, his knees coming down on either side of my waist as his hand comes to my throat again.

"Now, like I said, you're going to stop being a frigid ice queen, you're going to spread your legs, and you're going to let me fuck you."

I'm choking on a sob as I push out a hoarse whisper. "You don't want me."

"What does wanting you have to do with it? You're fucking mine, Bella. You, and your shares, and your seat on the board. All mine. Which means you will do as I say."

I'm gasping even as Preston eases back. "But I'm a man of reason..."

I stare at him. Gris has been silent and I don't even know if he's still on the line. That is until I hear the soft click of a car door.

And then the ding of an elevator door.

"What... what does that mean?"

"Why don't you go clean yourself up? Wash your face. And put on something pretty." Preston sneers. "You look like shit."

He wants me to make myself pretty so that he can force himself on me?

Through the phone, I hear the ding of the elevator again. Is Gris on my floor?

Preston pushes himself up and starts striding toward the bathroom. "Oh yeah, and you're going to have to call Mason and tell him that the wedding is back on." And then he closes the powder room door.

"Gris?"

"I'm right here, sweetheart." And then my apartment door opens.

Thank goodness.

CHAPTER TWENTY

GRIS

MY BLOOD IS RAGING in my veins.

I've kept quiet, because I know that Preston doesn't realize I'm on the phone. But I heard Arabella's cries, the words he said to her.

I am going to kill Preston Wingate.

I don't mean those words figuratively. I mean Killian and I are going to make him disappear. Gone. Vanished. No trace.

I walk into Bella's apartment, through the kitchen and around the island, and stop dead in my tracks.

She's lying in a heap on the floor, her face swollen and stained with tears, bruises blooming all over her body.

I'm not just going to kill him, I'm going to tear him limb from limb, scatter him so far across the world, they'll never be able to reassemble his body.

Without a word, I scoop Bella up in my arms and carry her over to the kitchen. She curls into me, her sobs muffled by my chest.

Here is the thing about me. I know how to play a fucking long game.

So, am I killing Preston today? No.

Am I going to whisper in that motherfuckers ear the pain that's coming his way… you bet your fucking ass I am.

"I'm just going to get you some ice, sweetheart," I whisper into her hair.

"I don't need ice," she croaks, and I know, just by the sound, that his hands were around her throat. Anger is surging through me, crashing over me in waves.

I set her down on the floor against the cabinet and do a quick inspection. Bruising on her neck, her face, her arms.

Sliding open the drawers, I get out two ice packs. The first goes on her neck, the second on her cheek. I lift her hands to hold both packs in place, and then I call Luke.

He doesn't pick up.

I call back.

Still nothing. I call again.

On the third go, he barks into the phone. "What?"

"I need you at Arabella's now." And then I hang up.

"He's with Mason," Arabella says her eyes sliding closed.

A bit of surprise slides through me. Maybe I should care that all of my plans on that front might fall through, but I don't. Am I going to lose tunnel access? My friendship with Luke?

I can't feel bad about either. All I care about is Arabella.

She opens her eyes again. "If Mason comes here, all my plans and all of yours could be ruined."

"Don't talk, sweetheart," I tuck her hair behind her ear. "I know you want to get your brothers back together. And I want mine to get access to the Kincaid tunnel. But that doesn't matter right now. All that matters is that Preston gets what is coming to him and that you are safe."

Her eyes widen even as the bathroom door swings open. We're crouched by the fridge, mostly blocked from the island and I stay down.

Does Preston think he's a big man, beating up a woman? He's about to find out how real predators hunt.

And how some like to play with their prey…

"Where the fuck are you, Arabella?" he spits. "I told you what was—"

I stand up. "Why don't you tell me?"

His eyes widen in surprise. "Lord Griswold? What are you doing here?"

"Just Gris," I take off my suit jacket then, folding it and placing it on the counter. Then, I start to remove my tie. "Why don't you have a seat, Preston."

"But… what… why?" He remains standing, looking at me with absolute confusion. Stupid fuck doesn't even understand he should be afraid. But I've got nothing but time, so I'll play along.

"What am I doing here? Well… let me see. Before you, I was in business with Kincaid. And by the way, I have first-hand knowledge of how, when Mason changes his mind, he pulls his support with barely a blink of an eye." I give him a wolfish grin.

He's still not getting it, as he gives me a conspiratorial eye roll. "Trash. All of them."

My teeth grind together. "But unlike you, I have developed a plan for winning their support back that does not involve beating up women."

He takes a half step back, his eyes growing wary. Finally. "I didn't know you knew Arabella."

"I've gotten very close to Luke Kincaid. He has been… concerned by your sudden entrance into his beloved sister's life. He's on his way now." I've begun playing with my food.

"I…" Preston starts edging for the door, sensing the danger. "It's not like that. A man has to keep his woman in line—"

I'm around the island with my hand at his throat before he's made it two steps. "Did you think you'd get away with this? That you could touch her and not pay?"

I push him toward the open-concept family room, as he stumbles and falls, crashing into the coffee table, which cracks into a hundred pieces when his weight lands on it.

"Shit man, I don't know why you care." He rolls on his side, trying to get up but he's slow. Far slower than me.

It's not fair. He probably gets all his exercise on his daddy's yacht. But me? I like scrapping. I've done it all. Wrestling, fencing, boxing, kickboxing. Helps release the aggression.

And I'm on him again, before he can even make it into a crouch. I pin him down, how I'm guessing he pinned Arabella. I want him to taste it. The fear.

I don't give him an explanation, instead I crack him a good one in the jaw, but I do grit out between clenched teeth, "You're going to suffer. I'm going to make you hurt like you've never hurt before."

He tries to fight but I outweigh him, out muscle him, outfight him, and I easily subdue him again. "But before I hurt you, I'm going to let Luke have a go at you." And then I ease back, with another smile that should frighten the shit out of him.

"What the fuck man?" He says, flexing his jaw. "What's she to you?"

I don't need to tell him shit.

But I look back to find Arabella standing there with wide eyes, ice in both hands, which have dropped to her sides. "Put the ice back on your bruises, luv," I calmly tell her. "And then come sit on the couch. You must be exhausted."

A knock sounds on the door. My brow furrows. That was quick.

"Delivery," a voice calls through the open crack in the door I never closed.

"Leave it in the hall," Arabella rasps, a few tears leaking down her cheeks, and then she does as I asked and comes to curl up on the couch.

She folds herself into the tiniest ball that both makes me ache and pisses me off even more.

Preston starts to struggle again, but I subdue him with a hand at his throat. "Hold still, you motherfucker."

He does, his eyes wide with fear because he knows what's coming. Finally, some sense from this fucking guy.

We don't have to wait long before the door swings open. "Why is there sushi on the floor in the hall?" Luke asks. I hear the crinkle of the bag as he picks it up.

And then I hear it hit the kitchen floor. "What the actual fuck?"

"What's wrong?" Another male voice asks. Mason. Fuck. The whole charade is blowing open now.

I knew this could happen. I can only hope he doesn't take up the fight with me so that I can't give Preston what he so richly deserves.

Triston is going to kill me if Mason doesn't do it first.

"Mason?" Arabella looks up, more tears leaking from her eyes. "I'm sorry."

I turn to see Mason's hands ball into fists. Who is he going to hit?

But before I find out, Preston clocks me with a decent blow across my cheekbone.

Didn't think he had it in him, and I might respect him slightly more, but it only gives me permission to bring my fist down, right between his eyes.

He's out in an instant.

I stand up and move to Arabella. I don't care if Mason is watching, the secret is out now, so, scooping her up in my arms, I sit back down with her curled on my lap.

She burrows into me again, curling so small with her legs drawn up to her chest, that I can fit my arms completely around her.

I drop my swelling cheek to the top of her head and hold her close. "I promise you. He'll never touch you again."

She doesn't respond, just nuzzles closer.

But Mason is glaring at me. I ignore him. If Preston was prey, Mason is the pride leader, and I am the lion encroaching on his territory.

And me and him, we're about to fight for dominance. There is no telling who might win.

CHAPTER TWENTY-ONE

ARABELLA

"DOES someone want to tell me what's going on?" Mason grits out, and I can hear his fury.

He never talks to me like that. Not usually, anyhow

I lift my head, meeting his gaze, which instantly loses a bunch of the anger, being replaced with fear. "Don't be mad, Mason." I can barely get the words out, but he hears them.

He steps over Preston, and crouches in front of me and Gris. "I'm not mad at you, Bellabear."

Each of my brothers has their own nickname for me. That was Mason's. But unlike Luke, who still uses his, Mason hasn't called me that in years. Not since before our mom and dad died.

"Preston did this to her?" Luke asks, standing over Preston with his arms crossed.

"Yeah," Gris answers. "He fucking did this." I feel the current of tension that runs through him despite the comfort of his hold.

And I feel how I always feel when I'm in his arms, only it's even stronger. I want to lose myself in Gris. Hide in him. I tried to play

Kincaid games for a hot minute, and now I'm a broken and battered bag of bones in his lap. I'm so stupid.

And I am going to give myself tonight, to lie in his arms, draw in his comfort. I'm going to give him my virginity too.

Because when he came striding through my apartment door, I realized that I loved him. I'm in love with him.

But I also know he doesn't love me back.

He's wants me. I know he does. And he does a much better job of faking it than Preston ever could. But I heard what he said to Preston, about having a plan to win Kincaid support back.

I'd be a fool not to understand that he meant me. I'm the plan. And he's doing an amazing job of making it all feel natural.

I don't get out of his lap. I just... can't.

"Is someone going to tell me why Gris is here?" Mason asks, sounding pissed again.

"No," I answer, my eyes closing. "No one is telling you."

"Don't talk," Gris slides his hands up and down my back. "Keep the ice on the parts that are swelling." Then he looks at my brothers. "I think a doctor should be brought in to examine her."

"I'll make the call." Luke pulls his phone from his pocket, and with a few quick buttons, he's speaking softly into the mouthpiece.

"And him?" Mason points down at Preston.

Gris gives a small shake of his head. "He'll be fine. He doesn't need a doctor."

No one argues.

Mason draws in a deep breath. "Is anyone going to provide any clarity on anything?"

"I saw Preston with another woman," I whisper. "He knew that I knew, and he came here to force my hand."

"This was his plan for getting you to marry him?" Luke scoffs.

"I'm guessing he also had no idea that Gris was in play," Mason tries again, looking at Luke.

"I'm sure he didn't," Gris answers. I lift my face to protest, but he gently runs a hand up into my hair, keeping my head on his chest. "And technically, I'm not in play. Just helping out a friend."

I give a small snort.

"Which friend is that?" Mason asks.

"Me. I'm the friend," Luke answers as he hangs up.

I groan. Not because of the pain but because the one thing I thought I got right is about to explode. I know it.

My brothers are about to break each other into a million pieces.

Mason is standing in a second. "Why would you put our enemies in charge of our sister?"

"First," Luke grunts back, "That piece of shit is the enemy, and you gave him an unlimited-access pass. And then Bella was ignoring my calls and texts. I needed a way in, so she didn't marry that fucking guy."

Mason shakes his head. "This was the plot she was referring to at dinner. The thing you did to her, that was like what I did to Kate."

Luke scrubs at his face. "It wasn't my best idea. But let's be honest, we all know I'm the worst at this game. Which is why you should buy me out, no matter what Bella says."

Mason snorts. "Fuck off." I tense, knowing my brothers are about to explode, until Mason lets out a long breath. "You did a better job of protecting Bella than I did."

I lift my head. Really? I didn't see this coming.

But then Mason points a finger at Gris. "But you are getting the fuck out of my sister's apartment, and you are never to see her again."

"No." The single word is from Gris.

He doesn't move, he's like granite underneath me.

"Look, fucker," Mason stares at Gris with hard eyes. "If you ever want a hope of doing business with me again, you'll walk out the door and never come back."

Gris is so still, I hold my breath, as I tip back to look up at him. He's staring back at Mason with unwavering strength.

Neither would hurt me.

But being caught between them...

I shiver and Gris automatically wraps me up tighter. "Gris," I say softly. "It's all right. Think of your family."

I'm giving him permission. And an out.

"Is that what you want me to do? Leave you?"

My body revolts before I can stop it, gripping at his shirt tighter. He still hasn't moved a muscle.

Maybe I should forget what I know. Pretend he might feel the same and sink into him. He'd take care of me. And the sex…

But what if he turns into Preston? Angry at being chained to a woman he didn't love?

I can't think tonight. I'm battered and bruised and exhausted by all that's happened. "Can we please talk about this tomorrow, Mason?"

"He needs to leave."

"He stays," I answer softly back.

Mason lets out a long, frustrated breath, but doesn't argue. Instead, he crouches down again. "I can't stand here and do nothing. Let me look at her."

Gris loosens his hold, enough so that Mason can turn my head this way and that, inspecting all the bruises. "How long until the doctor gets here?"

"A minute. Two," Luke answers. "Gris, maybe we bring Bella into her room so she can lie down? We'll bring the doctor in when he gets here."

I shake my head. "No."

"It's a good idea," Gris follows up, giving me the lightest squeeze. "You should relax, stretch out your muscles."

That sounds amazing but I'm afraid to let Gris out of my sight. "You'll come with me?"

"I think I might need to speak with your brothers."

Fear skitters through me. I need him in bed with me tonight. "Don't leave," I beg, tipping my head back. "Promise."

"I'm not leaving."

"Promise."

"I promise." He runs his thumb over my bottom lip before he drops a light kiss on my mouth.

I stare into his eyes for another five seconds, searching for the truth.

Finally, I nod. He lifts me into his arms, carrying me into the bedroom.

"Gris. Whatever they say, please say you'll stay with me tonight." I need his arms around me.

"I'm not going anywhere, princess." He kisses me again and then he gently lays me down on my bed. "I'll stay for as long as you want me to."

I barely bite back the one word that threatens to pop out of my mouth. Forever.

That's how long I want him to stay.

CHAPTER TWENTY-TWO

GRIS

I TUCK Arabella in and then head back out to the family room. But I don't stop at Luke and Mason.

Instead, I enter the kitchen, picking up the bag of sushi. Taking it out, I inspect the contents.

It's mostly salvageable so I place the container in the fridge.

"What are you doing?" Mason grumbles, his arms crossing over his chest.

I close the fridge. "She hasn't had dinner. I was checking her food."

"Food?" His eyes narrow. "You're concerned about her calorie intake?"

Luke's brows are arched as he stares at me too. I dust my hands, ignoring the silent question. So he asks one out loud instead. "You're really comfortable in her place, aren't you?"

Mason glares from one of us to the other. "So clearly you're involved with my sister, and Luke was already aware. I want details."

Luke lets out a long breath. "You've already guessed."

"Tell me anyway."

"I convinced Gris to romance Bella," Luke answers, turning toward his cousin.

Mason's answer is to pop Luke in the jaw with a quick right. Noted. Mason might not be as bulky, but the man can hit.

Luke goes down, nearly landing on top of Preston.

"Hey, while you're down there, can you see if Preston is still breathing?" I call over the island.

Then something happens I never expected. Mason laughs. "That was a good one."

I smile back. "I was serious. Kind of. I hit him hard enough, could be lights out. Which is problematic considering how much noise he made coming in here."

Luke gets up on his feet, turning to me. "How did you know how much noise he made?"

"Mrs. Gillette called me."

"Who?" Luke asks.

"Next door neighbor." I give them both a hard stare. "I thought you two were concerned for her safety. How have you not introduced yourselves to the nosy neighbor?"

Mason shakes his head. "Fuck off. Arabella is off limits."

I stiffen my spine and square my shoulders as Luke stands shoulder to shoulder with Mason. If they think they can take me down... "I disagree."

Mason takes two quick steps so he's just on the other side of the island. "I know the play. I fucking wrote it with Nia. But Arabella is *not* going to be your stepping stone."

"But you'd let that fucker," I wave in Preston's direction, "use her like a fucking Kleenex."

Mason grimaces. "I was never going to let the wedding happen."

"I know," I cross my arms. "Just like I know you planned to use Arabella to convince Luke to come back into the fold."

"I fucking knew it," Luke spits.

Mason gives me a wary eye, his gaze moving up and down me. "How do you know all that?"

I shrug. "We think alike."

He rubs his hand over his jaw. "Doesn't change the fact that I won't let you use Arabella."

"I'm not using Arabella," I snarl back. "And honestly, you're the one who should be receiving this fucking lecture."

Luke gives Mason a satisfied smile. "That's right. Out of bounds, Mason."

"Shut up," Mason snaps back. "You unleashed him on our sister."

Luke's hands go up. "He played it like he did with Nia. Dinner and sweet talk. Nothing more."

My lips twitch down as Mason swings a Luke again. Luke ducks it this time and comes back at Mason with a good shot to the gut.

I've always thought that my family and the Kincaids had a great deal in common, but never more than I do in this moment.

We like a good brawl too.

My family has been part of the aristocracy for the past two hundred years. But before that...

It's a well-known secret that we were hustlers. Criminals.

My great, great, great, great grandfather swindled the title. We don't forget it. We use that strength to keep us on top.

Mason places a hand on the island, hunched over with his other hand on his gut. "That's bullshit, Luke. The way he touches her, the way he knows his way around this place, met the neighbors, he's done all manner of dirty deeds with our sister."

Shit.

I know Mason. I know how he thinks. But he knows me too.

Luke turns to me, and it only takes a second for him to decide and then he's barreling at me with the full force of his weight.

Luke's a brawler and I don't have enough room to sidestep as he sends me crashing back into the counter.

I hear cabinets splinter, pain radiating through my back.

"You motherfucker," he booms as he gets me with a fist to the gut.

"Luke," Arabella's hoarse cry snaps my attention from Luke.

She stands in the entrance to the hall, her hands clasped in front of her face.

I push Luke off me, and I stumble up, surging toward her. In an instant she's wrapped in my arms. "I'm fine, sweetheart. I'll be right in. Promise."

Luke stands too, and I swear I hear his teeth gnash together as he preps for another attack.

"Leave it," Mason barks at his cousin.

But that's when another knock sounds at the door.

"The doctor?" I ask with Arabella still in my arms.

Luke spins to answer the door as I lift Arabella back in my arms. "You need to be in bed."

"I'm fine," she says, her voice sounding better. "The ice is helping."

"The doctor will be the judge of that."

I know this conversation with Luke and Mason is far from over, but it will have to wait. Bella's care comes first.

In fact, so many priorities are rewriting themselves tonight. Bella comes first. Period. But telling everyone...

But I don't think my life is going to be the same after this. If I'm alive at all. Like I said, if the Kincaids don't kill me, my family is definitely going to see the job done.

CHAPTER TWENTY-THREE

ARABELLA

THE DOCTOR EXAMINES me and declares that I did not sustain any serious injuries. I'm just relieved and ready to be alone, but Gris isn't done. He grills the doctor for a full fifteen minutes.

Even Mason raises his eyebrows at the length the conversation goes on, and everyone knows the best word to describe my oldest brother is… meticulous.

Finally, I'm the one who excuses the doctor. "Gris. Let the man go. I'm fine."

He sits down on the bed next to me, ignoring both my brothers in the doorway, and brings his hand to my hip. "You are far from fine. With every passing minute, those bruises get darker. I didn't hit Preston hard enough. I'm going to—"

"Speaking of, Dr. Matthews, would you do us the kindness of examining the man on the living room floor? See if you can revive him."

"He's the one who did that to you?" The doctor asks me the question and I give a quick nod, even as Gris's hand spreads out wider over my hip, like he's protecting me.

The doctor looks at Mason, and Mason gives him another nod of approval before both men head out the door to check on Preston.

Which leaves me with Gris and Luke. Great.

Luke leans against the wall, his arms crossing over his muscular chest. Gris sits taller, blocking more of me from view. I reach out and brush my fingers over his shoulder.

He looks back at me, skimming his hand up my arm, he cups my cheek. "Need anything, luv? Hungry? I put your sushi in the fridge."

I shake my head. I was famished an hour ago but now I don't think my stomach would tolerate anything more than broth. Definitely not raw fish.

He strokes his fingers through my hair. "Something else?"

"Want some soup, Bug?" Luke asks from his spot on the wall.

"Soup would be good. Thanks."

"Gris, mind getting her that soup? She likes the Thai place down the street."

Gris glares at Luke. "You seem to know where to go, I think you can handle this one."

"But I asked you."

"Handing me the real job again?" Gris grunts back.

I push at his shoulder. "Do not make this worse."

"He's the one who tackled me into your cabinets. It's going to be a full kitchen renovation. And while I'm excited to see your design, Luke is going to split the cost with me. Since he's the one who did the body slamming." Gris keeps stroking my hair, even as he glares back at Luke.

"Fine," Luke grumbles, "I'll get the Thai food."

He's gone and for a moment, I just lie there, my eyes sliding closed, as I bask in the feeling of Gris's hand in my hair.

He adjusts the ice pack on my throat, his fingers gently working over my scalp. "I'll get you cold ice in a minute."

"Thanks," I whisper, just enjoying the moment. The only way I'm sleeping tonight is in the circle of Gris's arms. "Every time I think I've extricated myself from Preston, he manages to worm his way back in, worse than before."

"How did he get in tonight?" Gris asks. His fingers are still gentle, but I hear the edge.

"I thought he was the delivery guy. I stupidly opened the door. I know you told me not to let him in. I just..."

"It's not your fault, sweetheart," he bends over and brushes a kiss over my forehead.

I feel tears pricking at my eyes again. "How am I going to feel safe after this?" Preston will go back to New York eventually. Hopefully. But until then, I'm going to constantly be looking over my shoulder.

"I'm not letting Preston hurt you ever again."

"Gris, you can't promise that. He could show up again, catch me in a hotel lobby the way he did tonight. Knock on the door when I'm expecting a delivery." Panic rises in my chest, but Gris's other hand comes around my face so that's he's cradling my head in his hands.

"You can come stay with me. As long as you want. We're going to need to renovate here anyway. And after, you can redo my place. It could use a woman's touch."

"Gris," the offer lodges in my heart, ridiculous hope making my breath catch. "Don't—"

"We could go to England. My family owns six different properties. Leave your family and mine here in Vegas. Just be us."

Blood rushes in my ears. "But your business, my family..."

He leans close, whispering in my ear. "Nothing is more important than your safety."

He might have detonated an emotional bomb the way all the reason in my brain scatters. I want to sink so deep into him, that I never surface again.

"Gris," Mason calls from the door. "Got a minute?"

I choke a bit. He can't leave now... there is so much to say. But he kisses my forehead again, his thumbs brushing over my cheeks. "I'll be right back."

And then he gets up and follows Mason out the door. I'd like to follow too. Find out what they're saying.

But I feel my eyes sliding closed.

CHAPTER TWENTY-FOUR

Gris

Preston is sitting with his back against the couch, his eyes looking dazed and confused. "Not dead?" I can't keep the irritation from my voice.

"No," Mason shifts. "The doctor revived him. Said that Preston likely has a concussion and he'd need to be watched tonight."

"Where is the good doctor?"

"Gone," Mason answers quickly. "Don't worry. He's paid well for his silence."

I give a quick nod. "How does Preston seem?"

Mason looks back at Preston as drool dribbles down his chin. "He's not quite sure where he is or how he got here."

"Like I said. Neighbor knows he's here. At least for tonight, he needs to go home and be tucked in his bed."

"Could have a concussion. He might die in his sleep."

Nothing would make me happier. "Again, if we're being honest, him dying tonight would be… problematic. At least from a culpability standpoint."

"You're a scary motherfucker, you know that?" Mason grins at me. "So what's the play?"

I reach for my phone and dial Killian.

This is a perfect job for him.

He picks up on the second ring. "Hello?"

I can hear voices in the background. A piano playing. "Are you at a piano bar?" My brother is a hard-drinking killing machine. He doesn't do soft piano music. He doesn't do soft anything.

"None of your fucking business."

That is Killian. And I should get to the point. "I need your help."

"Coming. Address?"

I pull out my burner and text his.

"How long until he gets here?"

"I'd tell you if I knew where he was coming from." I shrug as I watch Preston. The doctor is shining a light in his eyes, checking his reflexes.

"I'm going to have Killian take him home. Watch him. Make sure he doesn't die."

"That doesn't seem at all suited to Killian's normal skill set."

I give Mason a side eye. "Killian has a very methodical nature. He'll catalogue the details for later."

Mason gives a single nod. "So Preston is a problem you'll take care of."

"I will. Gladly. And in the meantime, I'm moving Arabella to my apartment."

I expect Mason to argue but he doesn't.

Luke comes back in, a bag of food in hand that he sets on the counter.

"Luke can stay with you until Killian arrives. If you two don't mind, I've got a long night ahead of me."

"A long night of what?" Luke asks, coming around the island.

Mason shrugs. "I'd like to see you both at nine tomorrow morning. Kincaid Enterprises."

Luke scoffs. "It's like being called to the principal's office."

"What's a principal?" I ask.

"A headmaster," Luke answers, before he waves to the soup. "Go feed Arabella while her soup is hot. I'll babysit the prick until Killian gets here."

"Thanks, Luke."

"Don't thank me," Luke glares. "I'm doing this for Bella. You and I are not done and we are not good."

I turn and head into the bedroom, but I see Mason speaking quietly to Luke before I close the door.

I don't know what they're discussing but I'm sure it's no good for me.

I don't care.

I meant what I said to Arabella. We can go to England, make a life there. I'm now the spare to the heir and my mother and eldest brother would like nothing more than for me to take up my place in English society.

It's not what I planned, but then again, I never planned to meet a woman like Bella, fall in love, and marry.

And I am in love. I can't deny the truth. Every part of me belongs to Bella and my driving mission has shifted irrevocably. Her protection is my first priority. Always.

I set the bag of food on the nightstand, Bella not stirring. Part of me thinks I should let her sleep, but the soup will soothe her throat, and food will give her the energy to heal.

"Luv," I whisper. "Time for supper."

Her eyes flutter open. "Gris."

"I'm here."

I get her to sit up, plumping pillows behind her back. Then, bringing the container to her lips, she takes several sips of the hot broth. "That feels good," she sighs as she takes another drink.

"That's good, luv. Keep drinking while I go get you a spoon." I hand her the container, and she holds it, taking several more sips.

My chest loosens to watch. She's going to be fine.

Heading out to the kitchen, I get the spoon, just as Killian comes through the door.

He's in his usual ripped jeans and tight T-shirt. "You were at a piano bar in that outfit?"

He scowls at me. "Mind your fucking business."

Luke grins, ducking his chin. "I'm Luke Kincaid." He sticks out a hand to Killian.

Killian takes it, appraising the other man. "Killian Smith. My family calls me Kill."

Luke's brows shoot up. "I've heard a lot about you."

Killian looks over at me, his gaze assessing. "This guy is why you know so much about the Kincaids, isn't he?"

"Gris been sharing our secrets?" Luke asks, sounding pissed again.

"No. Fucker plays everything close. Even with us." Killian shrugs. "Am I here to drop this guy off a pier?"

I roll my eyes. "We're not in London, Kill. There is no Thames and there are no piers in Vegas."

"There's a big fucking lake not too far away. Don't tell me my fucking business."

Truth. "Tonight, I just want you to take him home, tuck him in bed, make sure he lives through the night."

Killian's face turns black. "You want me to babysit?"

"Remember everything. You'll need all the details soon."

That makes my brother smile. Crazy fuck.

Grabbing a spoon from the drawer in the island, I start back for the bedroom.

"You really do know your way around this place." Luke gives me a glare as Killian makes his way over to Preston to play nurse.

I pause for one second. "I'm in love, Luke." The words, so simple, ring with a truth that settles in my chest.

"Her or Kincaid?"

I turn to him. Having this conversation in front of Killian is very problematic. "Her."

Killian, who has squatted down, looks up at me.

"Let me guess, you're going to marry her, make babies, control her shares."

"She doesn't have shares, remember? That is your decision, not mine. And, just so we're clear, I've told you my intent, my plans, before you make yours." I give the spoon a little jiggle. "She needs this."

"Fine. But in that meeting tomorrow morning, be ready to answer to me." Then Luke turns on his heel and leaves the apartment, slamming the door behind him.

Killian, never one to mince words, stands. "You playing them? Or us?"

"What the fuck is that supposed to mean?"

"You're slippery as a pig in shit," Killian grunts. "Where is the meeting tomorrow?"

My jaw goes granite hard. "Kincaid Enterprises. Nine."

"Expect Triston," Killian says, and then swings Preston into his arms like the full-grown man weighs nothing. "And I still want to go to Africa next month. This cunt isn't going to be a challenge at all."

I grimace but turn back to Arabella's bedroom. Triston, Luke, Mason, Killian... they are all problems for tomorrow.

I find Arabella still holding the container, the broth almost gone. Silently, I hand her the spoon.

"Everyone sounds angry," she says to me, her voice sounding far more normal then it did a few minutes ago.

"Remember what I said about going to England?" I give her a strained smile.

She lifts her brows. Dipping the spoon into the noodles, she takes a big bite. Silence follows as she chews, staring off into space. "Listen, Gris..."

My hand comes to her leg, because it sounds like she might be about to give me the speech. I'm about to burn down the world to make her mine, so I'm not sure I want to hear what she's going to say. "I'm listening."

"You don't have to do this..." She shakes her head.

"Do what? Didn't you ask me ten minutes ago to stay tonight?"

"Oh, I want you to stay," she says with a small smile, and I relax. "And I still want you to be the one." Her voice is quiet. "But you don't have to make me promises. I know what this is."

I lean over then, until my face is just a few inches from hers, my mouth close to hers. "You listen to me. Tomorrow, I'm going into a meeting where all of your brothers are going to want to kill me. And now, all of mine are likely going to join yours in plotting my death. So you had better promise me that I'm going in there and telling them all to go fuck themselves so that you and I can live happily ever after."

I catch the soup as she drops the container.

"Gris?"

"I love you, Arabella."

"I..."

I lean in and then place a soft kiss on her mouth. She trembles as I kiss her again. Setting the container on the nightstand, I pull her into my lap. "Tell me that you feel the same."

"Gris," she whispers, sounding pained. "Don't play with me. Not tonight. You'll wreck me."

"I'm not playing you. I'm in love with you. We're going to get married and make babies, really pretty ones."

A tear slips down her cheek as she looks up at me. "I..."

"We can leave Vegas, like I said. Live in England. Buy a villa in Italy. We don't need Smith Brothers and we don't need Kincaid Enterprises. It can just be me and you."

She burrows into me then, her arms wrapping around my neck. "Oh, Gris."

Is that good or bad? I hold her tight. Then she tips her head back and looks up into my eyes. "I love you too."

I kiss her then, her tears salty on my tongue. When I lift my head, her warm brown eyes meet mine. "Make love to me."

CHAPTER TWENTY-FIVE

ARABELLA

"SWEETHEART," he groans close to my ear. "You're too hurt tonight."

His hands skim down my back, the touch so comforting, it's enough to make me ache. I've always trusted Gris implicitly when it comes to my body.

It's like my skin understood before my brain, that Gris was a man I could trust.

Tonight he was at my side when I needed him most, I sent out a distress signal and he—

"How did you get here so fast?"

He grins at me. "Mrs. Gillette called me the moment Preston started yelling."

My mouth hangs open. When I called, thinking I was calling Luke, he was already on his way.

I don't ask him to make love to me again, instead, I kiss him. It's long and deep, my tongue sliding between his lips.

He kisses me back, the passion climbing between us, until he breaks away. "I don't want to hurt you."

"You won't," I say simply, I know any pain I feel will be nothing compared to the pleasure.

"Arabella," he groans and kisses me again. "You're killing me."

I skim my fingers over his neck. I know he's conflicted, but I'm not at all. I've never wanted to be closer to someone more than I do him. Right here. Right now.

"This is about me and you, correct?"

"Correct."

"Then I say we seal the deal, Gris. I want to give myself to you the way I've never given myself to anyone else before."

"Fuck, Arabella. How could I say no to that?"

That's the whole point. He's not supposed to say no. I kiss him again, slow, languid, but with plenty of tongue.

This man lights me on fire.

I'm ready to be consumed by the flame.

His tongue tangles with mine, his arms cradling my body. I barely feel when he stands and sets me lightly on my feet. It's not until he pulls back, that I make a small sound of protest.

He grins down at me, his eyes full of wicked intent. "I'm going to strip those little shorts off you, luv, and this seems the easiest way."

"Oh," I blush as his hands come to my waist. He catches the hem of my tank and gently pulls it over my head. My muscles twinge a bit as I drop my arms. He kisses along my collarbone, unhooking my bra and sliding it down my arms. He stops, tracing a few bruises.

I look away. I don't want to think about them, about what happened earlier. All I care about is him.

"He's going to pay," Gris whispers against my skin.

"He already did," I answer, grabbing the hem of Gris's shirt. "And let's not talk about any of that. I only want to think about you."

He shrugs his own shirt off and then pulls me into his embrace as he nuzzles my ear. "No man is ever hurting you again."

My eyes drift close as I tip my head back, his lips sliding up my neck. Gris is more than strong enough to keep me safe. Protected.

I reach between us, undoing the button of my shorts. "I know."

He smiles against my skin. "You do, do you?"

I slide my hands up his arms, stopping at his biceps. Gently, I give them both a squeeze. "But, Gris..."

"Yeah, luv?"

"Don't do too much damage to your family. Mine was already blowing apart, but I don't want you to lose yours…" I know what he's doing. If we leave, he proves to me there wasn't an agenda. He really loves me.

But I don't want to see his brothers hurt because of me.

He looks down at me, his gaze nearly unreadable as he reaches for the zipper on my shorts, unzipping them, before pulling them down over my hips.

My hands come to his shoulders. He squats lower, sliding the shorts over my skin as he leans in and kisses my hip. "Are you trying to protect my family?"

"I suppose that's silly, considering I don't know any of them." The shorts hit the floor, and he skims his hands back up my legs until he's holding my hips in his hands. He's still squatting down in front of me.

"It's not silly at all. I love how soft you are, caring. It's not a trait that's represented much in my family." He stands, letting go of me long enough to shuck off his own pants.

As many times as I've seen him without clothes, I still stare, my own body heating as my eyes travel down his perfect frame. "God, Gris, you're so…"

He's still wearing boxer briefs, but I can see his erection and I reach out, stroking him through his underwear.

I love the feel of him in my hand and I give him a small squeeze, licking my lips.

"Bella," his hoarse groan fills the room. "When you lick your lips like that…"

"I want to taste you," I whisper back.

I know what he wants. He wants to protect me tonight. But here is the thing. He already did that, right when I needed him most.

Now it's my turn to worship him. I feel it deep down, how much I want to give to him. My body, my heart, my time, and all my love. It all belongs to him. It's my turn to drop to my knees as I pull the briefs down to his thighs, his cock springing free and bumping right into my lip.

It knows exactly where it wants to be.

I flick my tongue out and give him a lick, a taste, before I wrap my lips around the head and give a small suckle.

"Fuck," he grits out, his hand coming into my hair.

But he doesn't pull me closer, doesn't use his grip to slide deeper into my mouth, instead, he uses it to hold me back.

I look up at him, my brows up. "You don't want to be inside my mouth?"

"I want nothing more. But not tonight. Not after what your body has been through." He pulls me back up his body, then lifts me in his arms and lays me on the bed.

Hovering over me, he takes my underwear off too, and then settles his shoulders between my legs. "So you get to lick me, but not the other way around?"

He gives me a one-sided grin. "Don't worry, luv, you'll make it up to me another time. But tonight, we're going to get you so wet, I'm just going to slide right inside you."

Those words cause a flood, my slickness starting to coat my thighs.

And then he reaches out his tongue, lapping at my folds.

My head arches back, and heedless of my stiff body, my hands bury into his hair, my toes curling as I spread wider.

He zeroes in on my clit, swirling his tongue over the little nub as two of his fingers slip inside me.

I'm already panting, my body spiraling upward as pleasure crashes through me.

I'm pulling his hair, pleading noises falling from my lips as he relentlessly licks at me just where I need it.

My insides are so tight, I feel like I might break, my heels now digging into his back.

He doesn't stop, or say a word, as his tongue pushes me higher and higher, his fingers pumping in and out of me.

With a loud cry, I break, the orgasm slamming through me.

He's up in a second, before I've even finished, his body skimming up my mine, as his cock settles into my soaking wet folds.

I wrap my arms around his neck, pulling him into a deep kiss, my scent all over his lips and tongue.

He rumbles into my mouth even as he sinks deeper inside me. I feel the stretch, the burn. But our eyes are locked, in each other's arms, as he moves with such a gentle slowness, that I don't make a sound.

I won't ruin this moment with tears or complaints. All I care about it the connection. "I love you so much, Gris," I push out with a deep breath, keeping my eyes locked on his. "I want to give you everything."

His eyes widen as he finally settles deeply inside me. "I love you too, Arabella. You're mine. Mine to love, mine to protect. Mine to care for."

And then he slowly pulls back out, pushing gently back in. I know he's keeping the pace easy and light for my benefit.

He holds me tightly, kissing me, as he picks up the pace. But I can tell by the cords in his neck that he's straining for control.

I love him even more for working so hard not to hurt me. I feel deep in my soul that my life is changing, that it's never going to be the same.

I can't find the words to tell him how much he means, or how much I want to give him, so instead, I lock my legs around his, encouraging him to go deeper, take more of me.

I can feel him tightening, getting closer, though he still keeps his strokes light. Easy.

"I'm all right, Gris. Don't worry. I can take all of you, baby."

"Fucking hell, Bella," he groans. "Do you have any idea what you're doing to me?"

Tying him to my heart? I hope. I kiss him again, and it undoes the last of his control.

With a few quick thrusts, he cums hard.

The feel of him inside me, the heat of his cum, it's this other level that makes me gasp in a breath, the intensity of my feelings, making me gasp out a cry. I've got my arms locked around his neck, my eyes squeezing shut as I burrow into his neck. "Holy shit."

"Yeah," he says, dropping his cheek to my forehead.

"Yeah?" I ask, suddenly feeling insecure. "Is that… is that how sex always is?"

He gives a stuttering laugh. "Not even close."

I relax at that. "Oh good. I got worried for a second."

"Arabella," he says, lifting up to hold my face in his very large hands. "I meant what I said. Whatever comes next. It's me and you. I want to spend my life with you. I want to marry you."

I nip at my lip. "I want that too."

"Good."

"I might just need a little time, though."

"Why's that?"

"I still need to cancel my first wedding."

He stares at me for a second before he gives a hearty chuckle. "Preston and Mason can take care of that shit. It's their mess to clean up."

"Not a bad plan."

He lifts up, sliding out of me. But when he looks down, he freezes. "What's wrong?"

"Jesus, Bella," he curses. "Why didn't you tell me?"

"Tell you what?" I look down and there is blood everywhere. "Oh. Jeez."

"Did I hurt you?"

"No, not really. I thought it was wonderful."

But he's lifting me again, carrying me toward the bathroom. "Let's get you cleaned up."

CHAPTER TWENTY-SIX

GRIS

I WAKE EARLY, the early morning light streaming in through the windows.

Arabella lays next me, the bruises even harsher in this light. She's still asleep and I don't move for a while, just holding her close. She needs her rest.

But at some point, I'll need to get up. I have to get back to my place and get proper clothes for today.

If I'm going into battle, I'm going to be dressed for it.

I meant what I said. My family is going to be furious when they realize that I'm marrying Arabella without any advantage to our business.

But I can't have there be any confusion in Arabella's eyes. I'm doing this because I love her. Everything else will be second to that.

She stirs next to me, stretching as she pushes back into the cradle of my body. I don't hesitate, my hand on her belly, I pull her close.

It's so strange. I never wanted to marry. Have kids. But now… the very idea of a baby in her belly makes my chest tight. My fingers splay out, possessive.

"Good morning."

"Good morning," she hums, sounding half asleep still. "Get any rest?"

"I always sleep best when I've got you in my arms." I skim a hand down her arms, hoping to soothe her angry-looking skin. I need to call Killian. Find out the plan for dealing with Preston.

But first… "I can't stay long this morning, the meeting at Kincaid Enterprises is at nine."

"What's the meeting for?"

I grimace into her hair. She doesn't need to worry about that. "I'm sure your brothers just want to know my intentions."

"Then I should come with you."

My body hardens as my hackles raise. I know her family would not hurt her, but it feels like a war zone, especially with Triston also joining, and I don't want her near that shit. "I think some ugly things are going to get said. I don't want—"

"No one knows my brothers like me. And honestly, if they get that nasty, no one is better at telling them to shut it than I am. It's part of the little-sister gig."

She turns over then, her front pressing to mine, her thigh hooking over my hips. If she's trying to soften me up, it's working. "Arabella."

"If we're going to be partners, we go into this like we are. And honestly, I want my brothers to understand it's me and you. They're going to need to see it."

It's not that she hasn't made some compelling points. "Members of my family will also be in attendance and I'm not sure it's the best place and time for you to meet them."

"All of your brothers?"

"Just Triston, I think. We're twins, actually. Don't know if I mentioned that."

Bella gasps, her eyes widening. "You have a twin? How could I not know this?" Then she frowns. "Will he not like me?"

"I think he'll like you just fine. But he can read me like a book. He'll know my allegiances have changed."

She kisses me then. "And you're afraid he'll be angry with you and unkind to me?"

"Maybe." Probably. And things have been difficult enough for Arabella the past few days. What I'd like to do is spare her some hurt and make certain she's welcome in my family. We're a hard enough bunch, without adding in the fact that Arabella is from a rival family, and I was supposed to use her for our benefit instead of making her my queen.

But she's throwing the covers back and sauntering naked toward the shower.

"Where are you going?" I growl out, following.

"To the shower. Coming?"

"Is this the part where I tell you that you shouldn't come with me and you do anyway?"

"Yep," she replies smiling over her shoulder. "Don't worry about me and your brother, I'm not intimidated by grumpy men. That, I've been well-trained for."

I follow behind her, staring at her ass. Which is fucking perfect. And I just know, I'm in so much trouble because, much as I want to, I can't say no.

We shower, which takes a long time because I've got my woman in the shower, but by the time we get out, I'm cutting it close. "I'm going to run back to my place and dress. I'll come back to pick you up in an hour?"

I don't live more than ten minutes away and it won't take me long to get on a suit.

She nods, and then kisses me, clad in nothing but a robe. "Hurry back."

Is she worried I'll linger away from her side? She shouldn't be. I'll be back before she can curl her lashes.

I get ready in record time and drive back to her place. Coming down the hall, Mrs. Gillette opens her door. "Lot of noise yesterday."

"Sorry about that Mrs. Gillette," I give her a wink. "Your call was very helpful."

She smiles back. "Good. You kick that other guy out? Never liked him. Stick up his butt."

"Isn't that the truth. And yes. You won't see him again."

"Good," she harrumphs, as she reaches into the pocket of her bright floral housecoat. She pulls out her phone, holding it up. "I recorded some of the noise if you need it for the police. Arabella's a good neighbor. Quiet. Goes to bed early. Doesn't make a lot of noise. But that guy…"

I give her a quick nod. I won't need evidence against Preston, but I don't need to tell Mrs. Gillette that. "Thank you. I'll let you know."

"You just going to kick the shit out of him?"

"Already did," I answer with another wink.

She cackles. "Good boy. I like you."

I chuckle too as I let myself into Arabella's apartment. She comes out of her bedroom, her hair twisted up in a neat chignon, her dress strapless, her bruises on full display.

My brows lift.

One slender shoulder raises as she shrugs. "You're not the only one who can strategize."

The dress makes a statement about what she's given since her return to Vegas and for the first time this morning, I think she might have been right about coming to this meeting.

She reaches for a light blazer, covering her arms and chest. "For the hall," she tells me as she does up the buttons. "My neighbors don't need to see all the bruises."

I nod, before I tuck her hand in my arm, leading her down to the garage.

We drive in silence, reaching Kincaid Tower in less than fifteen minutes. Entering the lobby, Arabella is immediately recognized, and doors slide open as we're ushered to the elevator.

That's when I catch sight of Triston. He's quietly arguing with the receptionist. "I can assure you, I am meant to be at this meeting."

I half turn, debating if my brother is an asset today or not. If he doesn't make it past reception, he'll be furious, but it will be one less ego in the room, and I can deal with my family separately from the Kincaids.

"Problem?" Arabella asks, even as the elevator door opens.

"My brother." I'm still trying to decide.

Arabella looks quickly at me and then starts for Triston. She sweeps back across the lobby with all the grace of a queen as she reaches his side, holding out her hand to him. "Mr. Smith, so wonderful to see you again."

"Arabella," he takes her offered fingers, his eyes doing a sweep of the lobby until they land on me.

I give a quick jerk of my chin. She leans over, kissing first one of his cheeks and then the other. "I'll take it from here, Rebecca," she says to the receptionist.

"But Miss Kincaid," Rebecca says, as she stands, looking nervous now, "he's not on the list."

Arabella waves her hand. "An oversight. No more." And then she tucks her hand in Triston's arm, pulling him toward the elevator without a backward glance at the receptionist. The other woman is worrying her lip as she watches them walk toward me. "But Miss Kincaid," Rebecca calls, "Mr. Kincaid is clear. No one goes upstairs for meetings but people on the list—"

Arabella doesn't glance back. "Mason will make an exception this time. I'll make it clear to my brother that this was my choice, not yours."

Triston gives her an appraising side glance. I've been holding the elevator open. Arabella walks past me, leading my brother between the doors. I step in behind them, the doors closing so that it's just the three of us.

"Rebecca is quite the watchdog," Triston mumbles.

"It's the reason Mason hired her," Arabella nods. "He does not like anything unexpected."

Then, Arabella lets go of my brother's arm and slides her coat down her arms, neatly folding the fabric over one arm. I see Triston's nostrils flare as his gaze skims down her torso. "I should have called you this morning," he says to me.

It might have been better that we talked first, but the last sixteen hours have been ridiculous. "Killian filled you in."

"Killian is not a reliable source of information."

Arabella says nothing as she looks between us, before she slides her hand into mine. I pull her closer, skimming a kiss over her forehead.

Triston catalogues all the details. He does far more dating than I do. He simply has more interest in playing house with ladies, at least short term.

So I know that he knows, I don't kiss a lot of women's foreheads. His eyes narrow. "I might as well ask. Where are we in gaining any access to the tunnel?"

I grimace as Arabella looks up at me, her eyes worried. We will lose a lot of money on our casinos without that access, and this was a job my family entrusted to me.

If I were playing at the tables, I would have lost big time.

I see Triston's fist flex, and I know he's understanding the truth. Arabella taps my arm, her light touch pulling my attention from Triston. "Let me help with that."

Her words are quiet, but her large brown eyes are filled with a desperate pleading. She wants to help.

I know that Arabella has been searching for her place in her family. And now, she'll work into mine. I want her to find herself, but not if it's going to hurt her. She's been hurt enough.

But I don't say any of this as the doors slide open into a large common workroom.

Mason is standing on the other side. His eyes find Triston first, and they narrow into hostile slits. But only for a second.

In a moment, his gaze finds Arabella, and his gaze goes from narrowed to wide-eyed. "You look even worse this morning."

"Do I?" Her chin notches. "I'm assuming you know Triston Smith?"

I watch Mason's gaze flicker, fill with indecision. I've never seen it before.

"Triston," he nods, sweeping his hand for all of us to enter.

Arabella lets go of my arm and steps out first, taking her brother's arm instead. "He'll be joining us."

Luke appears, along with Leo.

The office is buzzing, people bustling here and there. Most give Arabella a long, appraising look, before they hurry off. She's put herself on display and it can't be easy. But she keeps her head high as she leads Mason toward the conference room.

"I didn't know you were coming, Bella," Leo says as he sweeps his gaze down his sister. "This is Preston's work?"

"Not now, Leo," she shakes her head. "We can talk about him later."

"It's been handled anyway," Luke says, crossing his arms.

Leo glances around the office, his voice booming over the fifty employees currently in the space. "Everyone make themselves scarce." The people clear in a matter of seconds.

Leo is the tallest, most muscular, and angriest Kincaid. He could give Killian a rough go of it.

His gaze swings to me, and I'm certain that Leo is not going to let the topic lie. He wants answers. "Neither Luke nor Mason filled me in on the details. And I want them before we discuss anything else. Preston did this?"

"He did." I come to Arabella's other side, my hand settling on the small of her back. With her hand still tucked in Mason's arm, it brings us all together in a way I hadn't expected.

"Who delivered the justice?"

Mason clears his throat. "Gris came to her rescue, knocked Preston out. Killian—"

But Leo is stretching out his hand to me. I take it. "Good man."

I hear Mason let out a long breath. Irritation? Frustration? Does Leo's handshake mean that I found some support?

I might not be down and out after all…

CHAPTER TWENTY-SEVEN

ARABELLA

THE TENSION between the five men is thick enough to cut with an actual utensil. It's why I came.

They're going to need a reminder that this is a family matter and that the entire situation will require some heart.

I wasn't strong enough to be that person before now.

I'd run, I'd hide, I'd let them fight it out. Not today.

We're putting some of the past aside and we're moving forward as a family. And like it or not, Gris is going to be part of that family.

I feel Mason stiffen next to me, as Leo and Gris shake hands.

I know that Leo does a lot of things just to irritate Mason. Mason thinks that Leo is just difficult, but honestly, I think Leo understands the truth. Mason needs to be regularly challenged.

He's a man who competes because it's deep in his gut. I see that now, and Leo takes on a ton of that energy.

Then again, Gris is well matched for Mason too. In some ways, he's a better opponent for Mason. Because Leo fights with brute strength but like Mason, Gris uses cunning.

My fingers tighten on my brother's arm. He looks down at me with a grimace. I don't know if Preston was a miscalculation on Mason's part, but either way, recompense is coming all the way around.

The elevator opens, and my brother Roman steps out.

Roman is suave, sophisticated. Classically handsome, he doesn't have the same rough edges as Mason or Leo.

I turn to smile at him, but he stops dead when he sees me.

Yeah. I wore this dress on purpose, but I still hate the way my brothers' eyes fill with hurt when they look at me.

I don't want to hurt them, but I do need them to understand. We're joining forces with the Smiths again.

They're about to be my family, and by extension, theirs.

Gris's hand is still at my waist, and I watch Roman quickly assess the situation. "Gris," he calls, greeting him first.

Roman is as smart as Mason. He doesn't ask any questions, I'm sure he's figured it all out already.

"Roman. Good to see you again."

Gris lets me go to turn and shake Roman's hand but once he lets go, his hand is on me again.

I'm still holding onto Mason, and looking up at him, I quietly say. "Before we all meet, I need a short conversation with just the Kincaids."

"Bella," Gris protests. "That's not—"

I shake my head. I know Gris is ready to go into the conference room and fight. Threaten to leave it all behind.

And I appreciate that. It might even come to that. But for the first time in my life, running won't be my first move.

Gris gives a quick jerk of his chin, saying that he understands. I let go of Mason's arm then, taking Gris's hands. "I won't be long. I know you have important matters to discuss." But I have a few things for my brothers to consider before Gris enters the conversation.

Maybe I should have told Gris this was my plan.

But Mason and Gris aren't the only ones who can work hidden agendas. "Leo?" I ask. "Would you lead the way, please?"

I already know Leo is going to be on my side and I'm going to use it to my advantage. Leo is my Switzerland right now.

Luke is angry at Gris, even if they are friends. Mason is the one who cut Gris out to begin with.

And Roman? I can't say. We've hardly spoken.

I hand Gris my coat and straighten my shoulders. What I do know is that all of my brothers love me. I'm going to trust in that.

We enter the conference room with its U-shaped arrangement of tables. This is where Mason reigns supreme. Not today.

I stand in the middle, not bothering to take a seat.

"Arabella," Mason rumbles. "If this is the part where you tell me that we have to accept Gris with open arms, it's not happening."

Everyone stops as my arms cross, and I pivot toward my brother. "You will compromise on this one, Mason Kincaid. I'm not asking."

He narrows his gaze. "This isn't the place you tell me what to do."

"You are such an asshole, you know that, don't you?" I've got a few things to say to Mason and that seems like a great place to start. "At the point you started messing with my marriage, you lost the right to draw those distinctions."

I see the very subtle wince.

"I love you, we all love you, but if you continue to refuse to compromise, to scheme behind our backs, you're going to lose all of us." I point at Luke. And then Roman. And finally, Leo.

Mason's wince becomes far more distinct.

"Gris and I are considering moving to England." I see all my brothers react. Roman's eyes go wide, Leo growls from deep in his chest.

But it's Luke who huffs. "He's not leaving Smith Brothers."

I shrug. "Ask him yourself. But I'm telling you, he's the spare to the dukedom. Without the tunnel access, he'll cut his losses, and we'll leave." I know the reasons are more personal. "In a similar vein, if Luke sells, I don't want the shares. I'll cut from this family, and you won't see me again."

"Are you seriously threatening to leave the family if I don't give

Gris access?" Mason's fists clench and I feel both Roman and Luke draw closer to my side. The battle lines are being drawn.

"I don't agree with what Gris did to Nia. What any of you did..." I slash my gaze over them. "For men who say they love their women, you've been playing pretty rough with all of us."

I don't stop there, though.

"But Gris was loyal to you. If anything, you were the one who went back on the terms." I point at Mason. "You know I'm right."

I'm the one who tried to bring Mason and Luke back together. I still want that. But instead of pleading with them to get along, I'm threatening to leave the way Luke should have done months ago.

I'm going to give Mason a chance to make it right.

Mason draws himself up. "We can't trust the Smiths to help with our agenda. They come with their own."

"Oh please," I scoff. "Pot. Kettle."

I get a small laugh from Roman. Leo smiles. Luke runs a hand through his hair. He knows I'm angry with him too. "Bug," he starts, "You wouldn't really leave, would you?"

"You did," I point at him, and everyone goes quiet again.

I shake my head. "Don't get me wrong. I left too. Went to New York. But you're all about to have families. And Gris and I... we're getting married."

"Shut up," Luke rumbles. "How long have you even known..."

"Don't start, Luke," I hold up a finger.

"You can't trust he's not just working an agenda," Mason cuts in. "He's using you."

"He is the only one who seems to actually be protecting me."

Silence fills the room. I'm not going to tell them how I feel, or try to explain why I know Gris and I are different. "You can believe me or not. You'll each make your decision based on how much you trust my judgment. I accept that. And I'll accept whatever decision you make. Give the Smiths access to the tunnel. Don't. But just know, I'll make my decisions, and you will accept them as well. You are choosing whether or not to come together as a family or blow us apart, never to be put back together."

Dramatic? Maybe.

But the silence is deafening as I cross the conference room and open the door. "Gris?"

"Yeah, sweetheart?"

"You and Triston can come in now."

Gris comes toward me, stopping to place his forehead against mine. "Are we staying or going?"

"Going?" Triston barks. "Where the fuck would you go?"

"I don't know yet. They're thinking on what I said."

"Griswold Smith," Triston thumps his brother on the back. "I think we might need a meeting of our own."

"Don't bother," Mason sighs. "I vote to honor the original terms of the Smith contract."

"Nia?" Roman asks.

Mason looks at Gris. "Thoughts?"

Gris glances down at me, and then back up at my brother. "I think I might start with some groveling."

Several smiles greet those words.

"Wait," Triston is still thumping his hands on Gris's back repeatedly and hard enough, they're reverberating through me. "We're back to paying for the tunnel?"

Gris ignores his brother, bending down to wrap his arms around my waist, and lifting me in his arms. "Vegas, huh?"

"Vegas," I sigh. "No one is as surprised me."

He chuckles as he kisses me long and slow. "Don't worry, we're going to take plenty of vacations to England and Italy."

"And New York," I smile against his lips.

"Not too many," Luke moves closer. "I'd like to add an addendum to the agenda. I think we each donate two percent of our shares to Arabella, making her a ten-percent shareholder in Kincaid Enterprises."

"You're not selling," I gasp and then smile. Finally. I got through their thick skulls.

"No," he shakes his head. "But I am stepping back from my duties.

And with Roman involved in the charity division, we might need to restructure the hierarchy."

Mason lets out a frustrated moan. "Can we please not make any more changes today?"

Gris lightly sets me down and crosses to Mason. "So... we're going to be family."

Mason looks like he might spit nails, but he holds out a hand to Gris. "I'm an even worse family member than I am a business partner."

"I noticed," Gris shakes his hand. "But that's nothing new. The Smiths and the Kincaids have always had that in common."

I smile. They're about to have me in common. What a rollercoaster keeping them together is going to be.

But honestly, this was the job I was meant for.

CHAPTER TWENTY-EIGHT

ARABELLA

TWO WEEKS LATER...

I SHIMMY my dress down over my hips and then smooth my hair in the mirror. We're late.

Gris and I spent all day signing papers and meeting with lawyers. It's official. I now own ten percent of Kincaid Enterprises.

Luke joked that in one stroke of my pen, I had taken on a massive amount of debt.

But I know he was kidding.

Gris and his brothers agreed to honor the original terms and paid Kincaid a handsome sum to connect their casinos to the Kincaid Las Vegas tunnel.

I don't know how happy the Smiths are with the arrangement, but when I'm around, they play nice.

Gris swears its fine.

But I think I'll find out the truth tonight. Because tonight, I meet the duchess. Gris's mother.

Another wave of nerves crashes over me. I don't have the best track record with future mother-in-laws.

And I did not intend to be late tonight.

It's a family dinner.

And by that, I mean all of the Smiths and all of the Kincaids, along with their wives.

Even Jake and Nia are coming, which should be interesting. More likely awful.

My belly flutters with nerves again, as I lean over the bathroom counter to apply more gloss in the mirror.

That's when Gris enters the bathroom, fiddling with his cufflink.

He stops when he sees me, his gaze catching mine in the mirror. "That's some dress."

I run a hand over my silk-clad hip. I was going for Jackie O. It's silk, pale, strapless, but it's still relatively conservative in its cut and lines. "Don't tease me," I wrinkle my nose. "I'm nervous."

I cap my gloss, the ring on my finger catching the bathroom light. It's like the one Preston gave me in that it's a diamond, set in platinum.

But this one is a family heirloom. From the turn of the century, it's hand-cut for candlelight, the elaborate setting flaring on either side to meet the stone, encrusted with diamonds and filigree, it radiates beauty and warmth.

Or maybe those are just my feelings.

"I'm not teasing," he says as he moves closer, the power of his body making me tense in the best way possible. "You look like a woman who should be ravaged."

"Gris," I warn, even as a little thrill snakes down my spine. "We're already late."

"They'll wait."

"My dress," I cry, trying again.

His answer is to bend me over the counter, skimming the silk back up my legs. "I can't be held responsible for the dress."

"It's going to wrinkle," I gasp.

"You'll be more relaxed," he answers with a cheeky grin before he bends down behind me.

With the fabric pooled about my waist, he yanks my thong down my thighs and then dives in tongue-first.

The intense pleasure that zings through me makes me cry out as I clutch at the faucet.

I can't think, I can't breathe, and I definitely can't protest as pleasure radiates through my body.

He inserts a finger inside me, working me like only he can as I lift my hips to chase the pleasure.

I'm already close to orgasming, my body so tight, my toes have curled in my heels.

But he must feel that I'm pushing close to the edge because he stops, standing behind me.

I cry out a small protest but he only grins again, shucking his pants down his thighs.

His tie is still tied, tossed over his shoulder, his shirt buttoned as he sinks inside me, stretching me, filling me. Our eyes are locked in the mirror, but as he bottoms out, mine close.

He feels so good.

I reach back, stroking my fingers over his hip, wanting to feel more of his skin.

"Bella," he groans, bending down close to my ear. "You're going to make me cum in a flash if you keep touching me like that."

"I love your skin," I sigh back. "I can't get enough."

He rumbles in my ear, pumping into me, as he wraps his hand around my front, fingering my clit.

I see stars as intense pleasure courses through me. How does he do it? How does he turn me into this woman who doesn't care about anything other than his touch?

He manages to push even deeper into me, my whimpers of pleasure filling the bathroom as my legs tremble from the building orgasm.

My hair is pooled in the sink, my face twisted in pleasure as he pulls out and then quickly thrusts back in, sending me over the edge.

I scream as the orgasm rockets through me. But he doesn't pause. With almost punishing precision, he pumps in and out of me, several quick thrusts that have him spitting and cursing until I feel him break, his guttural moan hissed in my ear as he fills me with his cum.

We stay like that, bent over the sink, for at least a minute until we finally push up. "Crap," I mutter as I look at myself in the mirror. He's made a complete mess of me.

He only laughs. "You've never looked more gorgeous."

"I cannot meet your mother like this," I protest, my eyes going wide. My makeup is smudged, my hair a mess, and don't even get me started on the dress. I can't wear it. It looks like it was tossed into a puddle and then wrung out.

"Fix your hair," he kisses my shoulder several times. "I'll pick out a new dress."

"Something your mother will approve of," I call. "At least make it good enough that she'll remember my name."

Gris stops in the door again, and then crosses back to me. "She isn't forgetting your name, luv, and she's going to love you. She's been praying for one of us to marry for actual years. You are an answer to her prayers." And then he strokes my jaw, turning my face to kiss me.

He's gone a moment later, as I shuck off the dress and clean myself up, at least my face. I'm going to dinner with his family with cum on my thighs but I'm not worrying about that. I know Gris did it on purpose.

He comes back in with a different strapless dress, just as I'm reapplying my gloss. This one is a pale blue that is knee length instead of past the knee.

It shows more skin, but it should be all right. I don't say a word as he maneuvers it over my head, zipping it into place.

"Ready," he says, his fingertips sliding down my arm.

"Ready," I answer, the nerves still there but I can say this… the orgasm really helped to calm them.

Lacing his fingers through mine, we make our way out to the car.

Everything about this dinner feels so right. From the way Gris hands me into the passenger seat, to the way he holds my hand the entire drive.

And when we finally pull up to the valet station, the last ones to arrive at Cheval Blanc, my nerves give another flutter.

"Sweetheart," Gris murmurs, kissing my shoulder again. "No worries. All right?"

Lord, do I love this man. Everything about this moment is so perfect. "I'm fine. But thank you for worrying." I don't even know how to express how happy I am to marry him. All I keep saying over and over is, "I love you."

"I love you too." And then he kisses me, long and slow and full of the intimacy that has made my world so vibrant with color.

It's then that I realize we have an audience. My family and his stand together on the other side of the glass.

Our hands linked, we make our way inside.

And all my fears evaporate as an older woman leaves Triston's side and greets me with a wide smile. "You must be Arabella."

"Your Grace," I let go of Gris's hand to curtsy. "I'm so honored to meet you."

She waves away my formality and pulls me into a warm hug. "And I'm thrilled to meet you."

I hug her back.

It's then that I catch Mrs. Wingate out of the corner of my eye. I knew that Preston was still staying at the hotel.

She stares at us, her jaw locked, her gaze full of vitriol I thought she'd be happy that I wasn't marrying Preston. That I'd given back the ring.

Then again, I'm joining the family she most wanted an association with. And I, gangster's daughter that I am, will officially become a lady when I marry Gris.

Lady Griswold.

I don't care about that part at all, but I know she does. Turning back, I smile at my soon to be mother-in-law.

"Now tell me," she says as she gives me another squeeze. "What are we thinking about for the wedding?"

Gris steps up next to me. "Would you permit us to marry on the estate, mother? I've been telling Arabella how beautiful White Cliffs is."

The duchess's eyes light up. "Oh, that would be so wonderful. And, of course, you must all come stay."

"It will hold all of us?" Mason asks, his arm around Charlotte.

"Of course. It's been in the dukedom for eight generations. The house can hold the entirety of the nobility should it be necessary."

"How many bedrooms do you think the estate has?" Triston asks his mother, looking genuinely curious. "I never paid attention."

The duchess waves a dismissive hand. "Too many to count," she answers, looping her arm through Triston's.

I see my brother Mason's eyes spark and I roll mine. Mason is forever dreaming bigger. I think I might know what his next investment will be...

EPILOGUE

KILLIAN

"FOR FUCK'S SAKE, Kill, it isn't nice to play with your food." My brother Gris growls into the phone.

I don't answer. That's the thing about being in a dark alley, spying on a secret meeting. Talking isn't really an option.

So I don't.

Though, to be fair, I might not have answered anyway. I'm a do-what-I-want kind of guy.

"Are you going to eliminate this problem or not?" he rumbles. "I'll do it myself if you're not up to the task."

He's baiting me. That's brotherly love for you. We both know of the two of us, I'm the killer. Not him. It's in my fucking name for fuck's sake.

That's when I hear his fiancé, Arabella, give a sleepy call. "Is everything all right, Gris?"

"It's fine, baby." My brother sounds like a fucking twat, the way his voice takes on this coddling tone when he talks to her. "Are you cold? I'll be right there to warm you up."

"Jesus," I whisper, rolling my eyes in the dark.

"Are you judging me, you crazy fuck?" I hear a door open and close on the other end of the line, he's clearly moving to another room. "You're supposed to get rid of Preston Wingate. Stop fucking around and get it done."

I hang up.

I don't answer to Gris, but he ought to know, I always do my job.

In front of me, I watch the weekly scene play out.

That fuckwad, Preston Wingate, takes a large bundle of money from a very tattooed, very large Russian.

I lean against the wall, watching it all go down.

I'm not playing with my food.

Not at all. Preston Wingate is a problem that's about to solve itself. He's mixing with the Russian Bratva here in Vegas, attempting to sell Kincaids' secrets.

I'm a crazy motherfucker and even I wouldn't dare make an alliance with the Russians.

On the bright side, these Bratva assholes are for sure going to kill Preston themselves. I've listened in to several of these meetings and Preston doesn't actually know anything of value and the Russians are getting pissy as he continues to take their money.

"You told us that last time," the one I believe is named Alec spits at Preston. "And it isn't anything we couldn't discern from public record."

Preston is shifting, his pasty fucking face getting even paler. "That's right, motherfucker," I whisper. "Dance like the bitch you are."

It's not that I mind killing. But Preston isn't even a challenge. Stupid, weak, I could have killed him a hundred times in the last two months. But it would be boring.

And besides, these Russians are shaping up to be the real hunt and the longer Preston lives, the more I learn about my family's newest enemy.

I already knew they liked this piano bar. One of them is some sort of fucking savant, and he comes here to play. I was scouting out the place and watching the Russians after they stole a deal on a casino right out from under us.

But my attention on the Russians had been diverted when my brother Gris decided to take Preston's fiancé, Arabella Kincaid.

I've got to be honest, Preston was almost smart. Almost. Marrying the Kincaid princess might not have given him access to their secrets, but it would have given him control of Arabella's shares and a seat on the Kincaid board.

We are making money hand over fist in Las Vegas, but the Kincaids… they are the current kings. Not for long…

I digress. Preston got cocky, thought he had the girl in the bag, and got himself a sidepiece before the wedding had even happened.

Enter my brother. Gris is the kind of handsome that makes girls go crazy. Preston Wingate never stood a chance. In a matter of days, Gris had broken up the engagement and claimed Arabella for himself.

That part that shocks me is how sincere he seems about her. She must have a magic pussy.

None of us are men with a lot of emotional depth. Me least of all, but that's a completely different and really fucked up story.

What matters is that when Arabella broke up with Preston, he beat the shit out of her. And people think I'm a sociopath.

That's when Gris decided that Preston had to die.

Imagine my luck when my two projects—the Russians and Preston Wingate—became a two-for-one.

And the fact that they'll kill Preston, while I learn how to take them out? Could the situation get any better?

But that's when I hear the door from the restaurant and into the alley rattle. Fuck.

One of the staff must be taking out the trash.

The Russians are ruthless and anyone who gets in their way disappears.

Which is fine by me, as long as it's not her.

There is this one waitress who I can't help but watch every time I'm here. It's the way she moves, the sound of her voice, the curve of her smile. Chloe, is what the other waitresses call her.

I still haven't decided if I want to fuck Chloe or dirty her up in far less wholesome ways, but I have no intention of letting these fucking Russians put their hands on her before I decide.

The Russians melt into the shadows and Preston ducks behind the dumpster.

A cook comes out, whistling as he goes, tossing two large bags up and over the side.

The sound of them hitting the bottom echoes through the alley, as the cook goes back inside, locking the door behind him.

As for me…

I've seen enough. If the Russians don't take care of Preston in the next week, I'll do it myself.

I don't need Preston to keep an eye on the Russians. I can do that from the piano bar.

And then I can keep an eye on Chloe too. What did Gris say I was doing? Playing with my food?

A salacious grin tugs at my lips. Yeah. That sounds about right. When it comes to my little waitress, I think it's… Game. On.

Gris and Arabella have finished off the "Lords of Las Vegas" series! But don't worry! I've created a yummy prequel novella for you to enjoy for FREE! Just follow the link, join my newsletter, and the novella is yours. King Daddy

But that's not all! The world will continue with Killian Smith. It's going to get darker and sexier, as we dive into the Smith family. "The Kings of Las Vegas" are coming to you late this spring!

Find out what happens with Killian and Chloe in: King of Depravity

KING OF DEPRAVITY

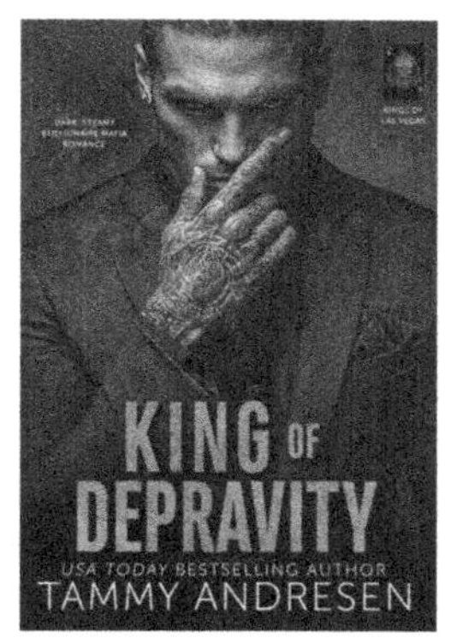

Chloe

"Sweetheart," some swinging dick from the corner booth waves a hand at me. He's like most guys in this place with his slicked back hair, expensive Italian loafers and a gut hanging over his equally expensive belt from too much pricey bourbon. "Another round."

"Of course," I smile and nod as I turn and hustle to the bar. Mike is working tonight and he's one of my favorite bartenders because instead of also being a jerk, he's funny. "Hey Mike, two more Macallan's, please."

"12?" He responds with a wink.

"Oh no, those guys only drink it if it's been aged 18." I smile back.

He shakes his head with a low whistle. "Good tips for you tonight."

I hope so. I need them. While the spring semester is almost over, I've got one more to go in the fall. I have to pay monthly in order to cover the costs my scholarship doesn't cover, so it basically means I'm always making payments to the school and my next payment is due next week. And that's the late deadline.

I set the snifters of bourbon on my tray, and straighten my fitted black oxford, smooth back my tight ponytail, before I plaster a smile on my face.

My black dress pants are painted on as I traverse the large room in my stilettos. They hurt like hell, but I get better tips when I wear them.

In the corner, the regular piano player stands, inviting one of the 'guests' to play a song. I've heard the guy before.

A tatted-up Russian, one of the other girls told me that all the tattoos on his fingers are because he's Bratva.

I don't care what he is, his whole table tips well. And usually, I wait on them as often as I can.

One of the Russians makes a habit of grabbing my ass, and he slipped me his number a few weeks ago, so I've been hanging back, letting other girls serve their drinks. I'll have to wait until he's lost interest.

It's hurt my bottom line, but I know better than to get mixed up with guys like that.

So instead, I serve the Macallan to the two middle aged swinging dicks.

The music begins, the Russian truly special on the piano, his skill so far above any of our players.

I'd like to stop and listen, but instead I lean over the table, setting the first glass to the guy on the inside corner of the booth.

That's when his friend places a definite hand on my ass.

I don't react.

I don't do anything but keep smiling.

I'm not above allowing a guy to cop a feel so that he leaves me a good tip. But that is where I draw the line. They can go home and screw their wives. I'm not for hire.

But as he gives my right cheek a big squeeze, I straighten, adjusting away, as I place his Macallan in front of him. "Here you go, sir."

"Thank you, darlin'," he drawls, his face already a bit ruddy from the liquor. "Tell me something," he starts, leaning closer with a look of hunger in his eyes. "You looking for a good time?"

Crap. These situations have to be handled delicately so as not to make the customer feel bad and stiff me from my tip. "Serving you gentlemen drinks is plenty fun," I say with a husky laugh, before I turn and go, leaving both of them also laughing in my wake.

I've got a mezzo soprano tone to my voice and I know lots of guys dig it. My hair is a dark honey blonde, and my eyes are green, but my skin has a sun kissed bronze to it, thanks to my mom's Mediterranean heritage.

Coupled with a generous backside, I get my fair share of male attention. Not that I date. I don't. Ever.

I'm too busy, and even if I wasn't...

Shaking off these thoughts I keep working the room, serving drinks as the night grows later and the patrons more drunk.

I bring a round of vodka to the Russians when Callie has serve a group in one of the private rooms. My stomach flutters but I push my nerves back down as I approach the table.

The one who asked me out, I think his name is Alexander, gives me a long heavy stare, his tattooed fingers flexing around his glass, as I keep my smile as generic as possible.

That's when the hair on the back of my neck stands up.

I straighten. My instincts are always dead on and I can sense that danger is close. Scanning the room, I catch the shadowed gaze of a lone man in the dark corner of the room.

I hate that guy. I don't know his name. I never wait on him, but he's here nearly every night. Sometimes he only stays for a bit, sometimes all night.

The other waitresses say that he doesn't drink much but he tips really well, as they giggle about how gorgeous he is.

I don't give a shit about his looks, the guy still creeps me out, which is why I usually give his table to the next girl in the rotation. Even I'm not desperate enough to interact with him for good tips.

He looks at me now, his dark eyes empty and unreadable. I know that look.

It's the look of a man that has no soul, that will hurt anyone or anything not out of malice, but out of joy.

That's the scariest mother f-er of them all.

He raises his glass to his lips and I catch the tattoos that cover his massive hands. He's tattooed like the Russians?

Come to think of it, he only seems to stay when they are here. I shake my head, sure I don't care. The less I know about that guy the better.

But that's when Alexander slides out of the booth and stands next to me. I mean right next to me. Like there is barely an inch between us. He drops his head low, his hot breath against my neck and ear. "You didn't call."

My smile slips as I duck my head. I'm tempted to tell him that I lost his number, but that only pushes the problem down the road.

Instead, I shift the tray to my left hand, sliding away from him, and placing the little plastic disc between us. "I should have told you when you gave me your number, but I don't date patrons of the bar. It's…" I'm searching for the appropriate word. It's not nepotism because I am in no way powerful.

But it's not good for business either. "It's against the bar's policy," I finally manage to come up with an excuse, looking up at him with an apologetic smile.

His eyes narrow as he reaches for my tray, moving it out of the way so he can step close again. "You need to understand, printsessa," he says in his thick accent, "that I am a man who gets what I want."

I swallow down a lump. He needs to understand that this isn't happening. Ever. "I can sense that about you," I murmur and he gives a low, appreciative laugh. "But my boss would fire me." And then I give him my most vulnerable eyes, the ones that ask for forgiveness as my lower lip juts out the smallest bit. "I really need this job."

He eats it up. I can see him shifting to be both sympathetic and appeased. It's not his lack of appeal, but my circumstances that kept me from calling.

My mom can make nearly any man do anything she chooses. It's disgusting. She's on husband number four, and this one is going to stick. Rich and drunk most of the time, she has unlimited access to his credit cards.

I will never be like that. I've promised myself this over and over. But I do understand the principles of what she does, and I occasionally use them to keep myself out of trouble. That's it.

He eases back into the booth, and I start hustling away. That's when dark and dangerous in the corner meets my eye again and raises his hand to beckon me over.

My heart stops for a second.

I'm normally way more careful about not meeting his eye, but the Russian had me flustered.

With a gulp, I make my way over to him. "Can I help you, sir?"

He leans over the table, out of the shadows and my breath catches. Holy shit, he's even better looking up close.

It's not that every feature is perfect. But every part of him works together to create this beautifully masculine man from the crook in his nose, to his cut jaw, to the bulging muscles highlighted by the fine cut of his dress shirt.

His dark hair waves back from his face, straight line of his brow. Only his eyes give him away.

They do not sparkle with anything. They're devoid of light, making him look almost... dead.

I take a half step back, swallowing down a lump, realizing he's assessing me too and has not answered my greeting, so I repeat it. "Can I help you sir?"

"What did that man just ask you?" his voice is a low gravelly baritone with a rich English accent that doesn't disguise his words are not a request. They are a demand.

I bring drinks with a smile and without question. I do not gossip about patrons with other patrons. "Sir, I don't think—"

His hand shoots out to capture my wrist. His grip is just tight enough that I feel his power, know that he could hurt me whenever he chooses. "Tell me what he said."

I hesitate for another second and he tightens the grip, my whole body tensing as I ready for the pain. "He asked me out."

"And what did you say?"

I shake my head like this is crazy, because it is. Not that I don't know crazy, or how to handle it. "I said what I always say, no thank you."

His grip loosens, but he doesn't let go as his thumb strokes along the inside of my wrist.

I'm so over stimulated from the whole interaction that my skin breaks out in goose pimples from his touch. "And if I asked you out? What would you say?"

"No thank you," it's out in a rush betraying my true feelings and not at all in keeping with my normal façade.

He gives me a grin and it's positively wicked. I cringe away. "And if I told you that I don't take no for an answer?"

"That's what he said too," I whisper, knowing that I am doing a much worse job of handling this conversation, than I did the last.

Maybe it's been too much maneuvering through male attention, or maybe this guy unsettles me like no other.

But his lips thin over his teeth as he tugs me down closer, bringing my face right to his face.

His scent wraps around me, and I have to be honest, he smells delicious. It's cedar and spice, with a hint of male musk that makes my heart beat a little faster. Or maybe that's just fact that he's got me bent over the table. "And how did you answer?"

"My boss doesn't allow me to date patrons."

He finally lets me go. "Is that what you're going to say to me too?"

I jerk my chin in the affirmative.

Reaching into his back pocket, he pulls his wallet out from and lays three hundred dollar bills onto the table. "You are waiting on me the rest of the night. Bring one whisky every hour, water in between."

I pick up the bills, slipping them into my small apron as I turn to do as he's bid.

"Chloe."

That makes me stop dead in my tracks. How does he know my name? We don't wear nametags.

I glance back over my shoulder, showing him my profile without making eyes contact. "Yes?" My voice is barely a whisper.

"You can try to deflect. You can run. You can even hide. But you will bend to my will, luv. I don't take no for an answer."

Fear steals my breath and for a moment I don't move. Then, I unstick my feet from the floor and scurry toward the bar, trying not to break out into a full run.

My instincts are never wrong and that guy is a psycho.

Want to read more? *King of Depravity* can be found on Amazon!

MORE ABOUT TAMMY

Tammy is the writer of Bestselling Regency Romance who could not resist the urge of writing in the dark and delicious world of Contemporary Dark and Steamy Billionaire Romance.

She lives with her husband and three children in Massachusetts and her favorite adventures are the ones that are found in books but occasionally she lives a few of her own!

Made in the USA
Las Vegas, NV
09 June 2026

48460173R00105